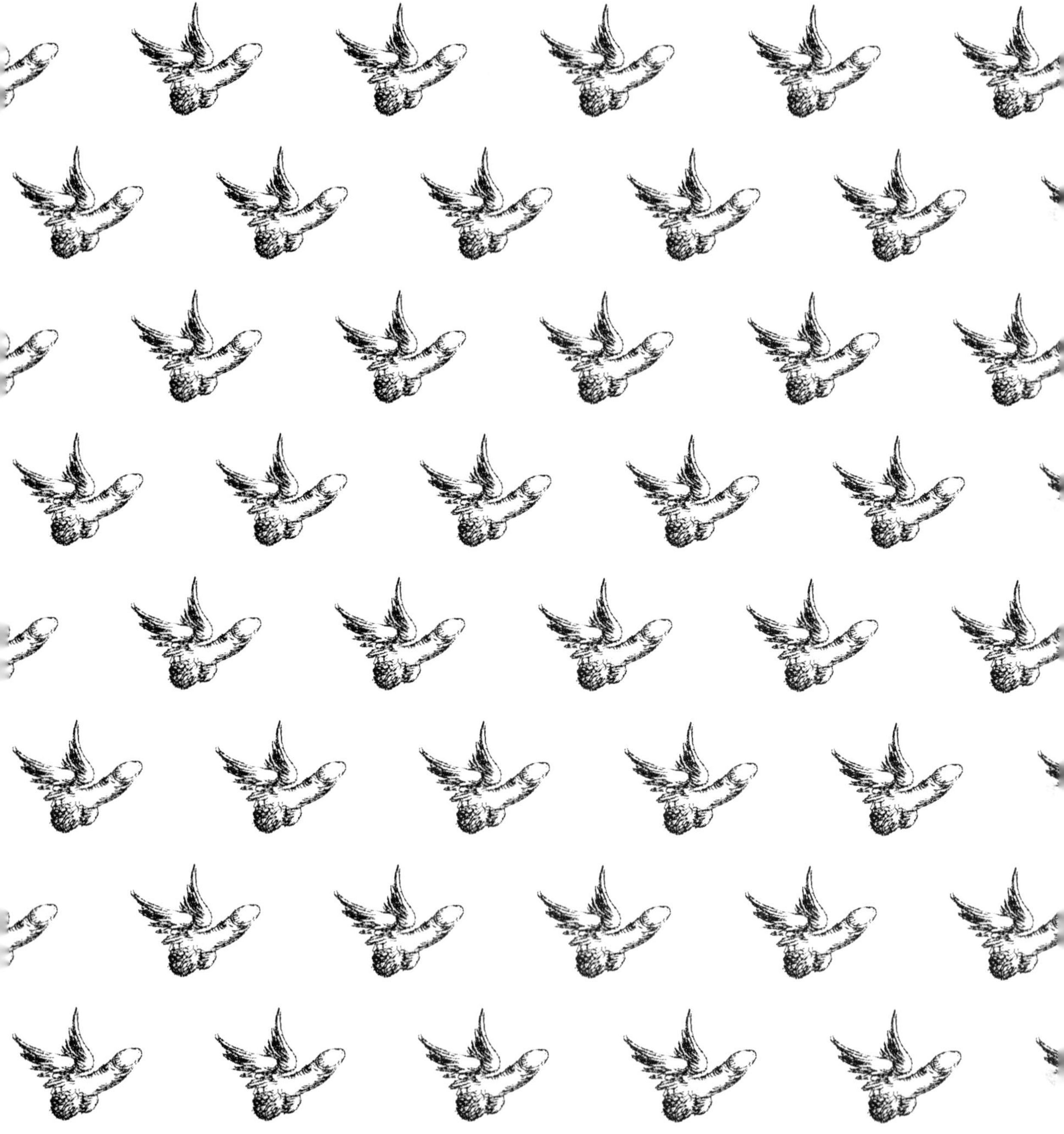

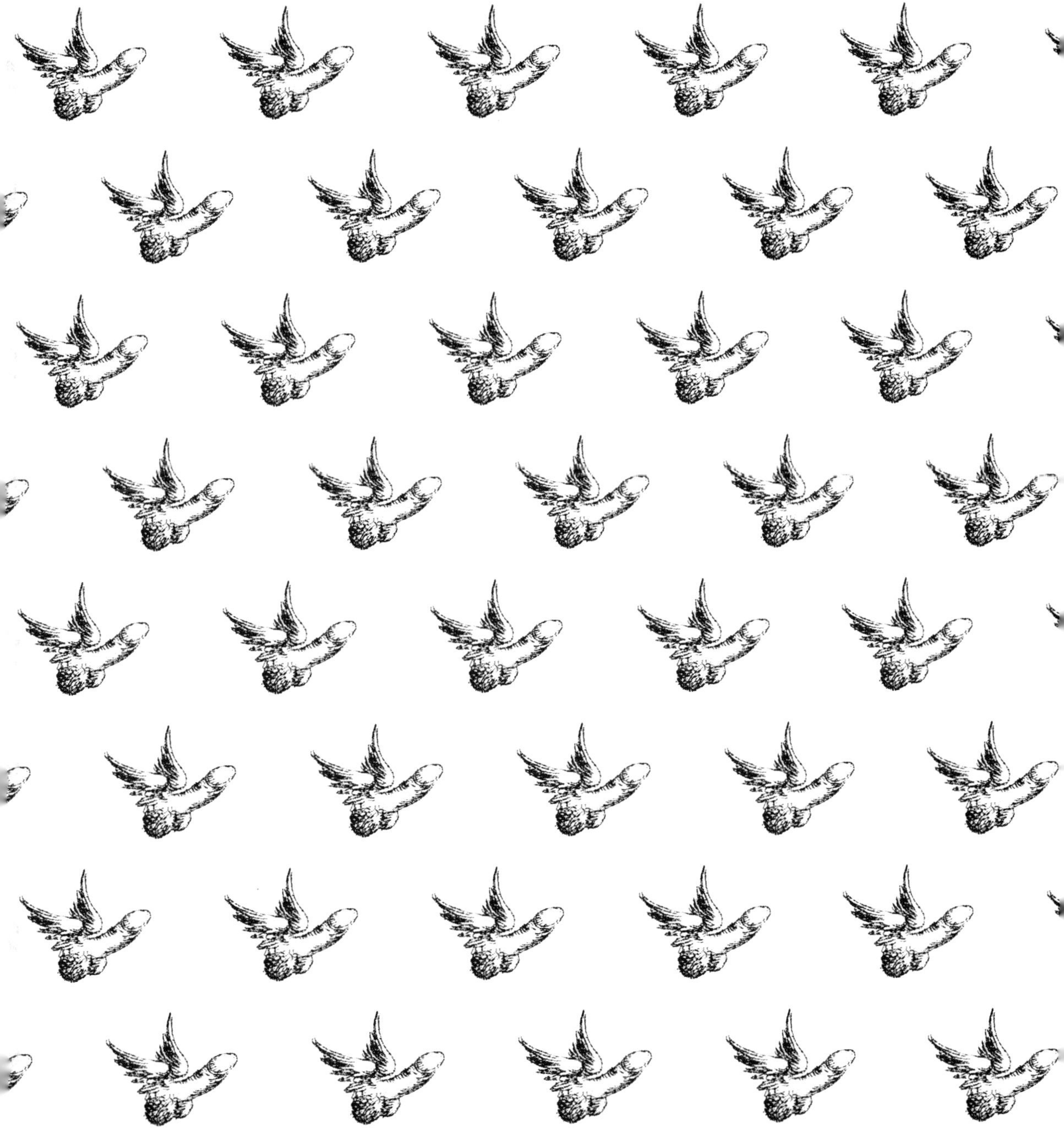

Bawdy Tales & Trifles of Devilries for Ladies & Gentlemen of Experience

Illustrations by Eugène Lepoittevin

Bawdy Tales
& Trifles of Devilries
for Ladies & Gentlemen of Experience

ISBN: 9781627311199

Determining authorship of scurrilous bawdy writing is challenging; many of the pieces included are the product of an, ahem, oral tradition. This exact collection is the product of long hours of research and has been edited for clarity and readability and thusly copyrighted by Feral House.

Feral House
1240 W Sims Way #124
Port Townsend WA 98368

Design by designSimple.com

Young woman, please listen my dear;
Armageddon is ever so near,
And we're going to win,
So you might as well sin,
And have fun with the devil right here!

Those Dirty Little Devils

By Sarah Lea Burns, Ph.D.

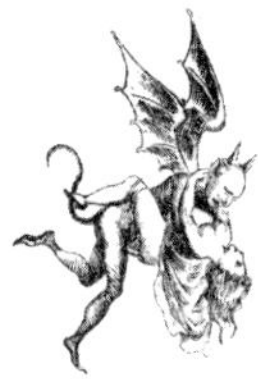

Little known today, Eugène Lepoittevin's 1830 *Charges et Décharges diaboliques* (and its subsequent variations) was wildly popular in France up to 1845, when, on April 29th, the Assize Court of the Seine seized and destroyed as many copies as could be rounded up. Deemed an affront to public decency—or, to put it more bluntly, outrageously obscene—Lepoittevin's album of twelve lithographic plates portrays the lewd pranks and antics of devils, horny hordes of them, as they assault, seduce, tempt, trick, and torment bevies of young damsels, who more often than not seem to welcome rather than repel their attackers' diabolical attentions. Of course, in this era of #MeToo, we might hasten to condemn Lepoittevin's imagery for the sadomasochistic relish with which his demons assail their defenseless victims—except for the fact that said victims are for the most part eager participants, intent on their own pleasures.

When Lepoittevin published his first portfolio of lusty vignettes (with several more to follow), he was only twenty-four years old and on the threshold of what would be a long, successful, and eminently respectable career as a landscape and genre painter, over the years showing 150 highly accomplished paintings, all told, at the Paris Salon, the official and enormously prestigious annual exhibition of the Ecole des Beaux-Arts. What on earth was he thinking when in 1830 he decided to plunge into rank (but hilarious) devilish pornography? For one thing, obviously, Lepoittevin, a skilled lithographer, figured he could make some money on the side, given the predictable demand for his product. For another—and more importantly in the contemporary context—the longstanding French governmental censorship of press freedom had suddenly vaporized with the success of the 1830 July Revolution that compelled the abdication of Charles X and elevated the so-called Citizen King, Louis-Philippe, to the throne as a constitutional monarch. Until 1835, when censorship clamped down on free expression once again, printmakers and their publishers enjoyed carte blanche to produce even the raunchiest imagery, public decency be damned. Why not push that freedom to a comical extreme?

We are learning about the ways in which prints like Lepoittevin's circulated through a network of printers, and bookshops ran underground enterprises selling pornographic material under the counter and relying on word of mouth rather than advertisement to attract buyers. A work like Lepoittevin's would have been announced to the shop's private clientele and presold via subscription, not unlike modern online fundraising websites. That the majority of purchasers were men is a great deal more than likely, though this doesn't rule out the prospect that women too could have gained access to the plates by, for example, purloining the keys to bookcases or cabinets where forbidden smut would be locked away.

To the extent it's been possible to determine, Lepoittevin was the first artist to come up with the idea of devil porn, inspired, perhaps, by the 1828 publication of Eugène Delacroix's lithographic illustrations to Goethe's *Faust*, featuring Faust's nemesis Mephistopheles as a beguilingly diabolical malefactor. Probably a certain measure of anti-clericalism went

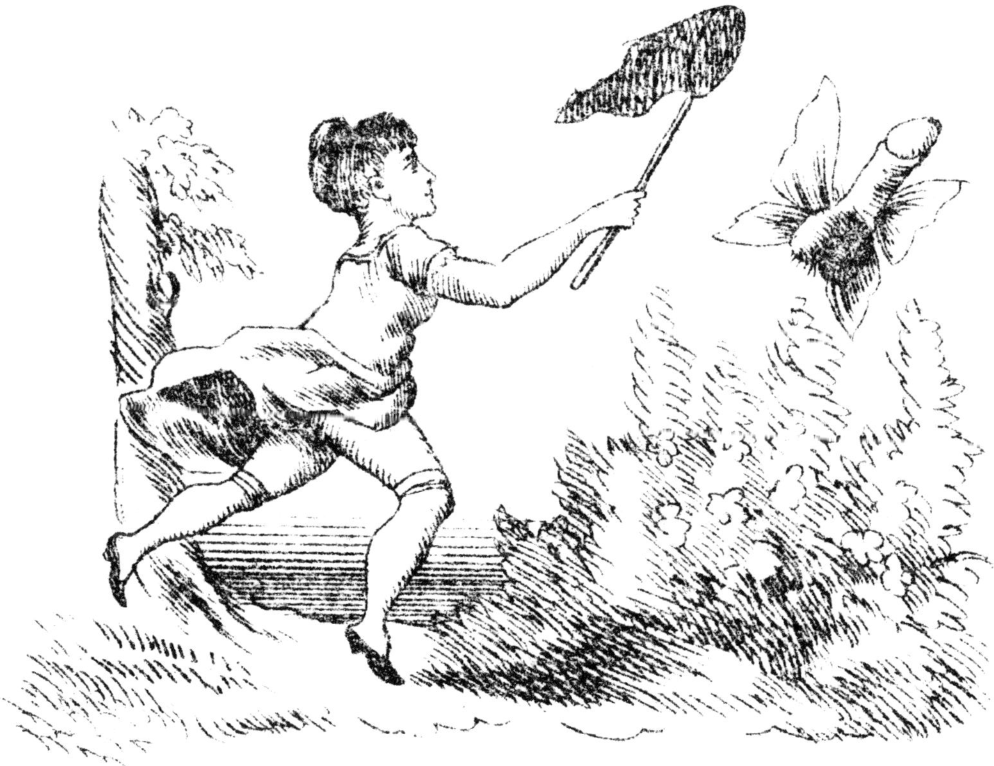

Le Joli Papillon

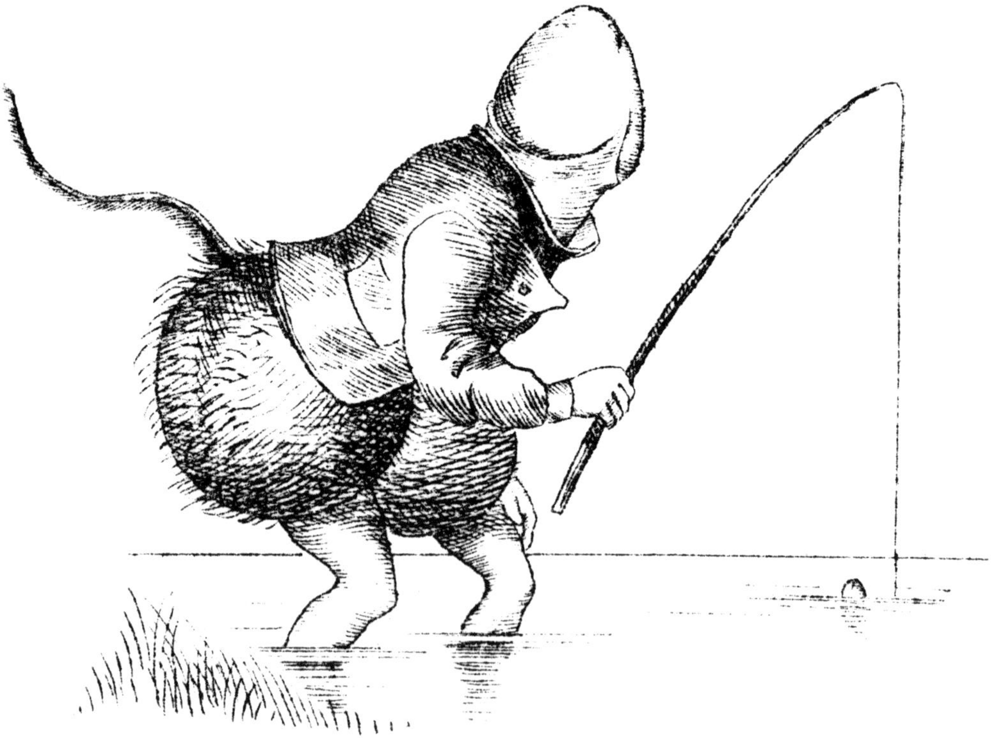

V'la que ça mord !

into the mix, too. In 1830, Lepoittevin also published *Souvenirs Patriotiques*, a series of lithographs celebrating the July Revolution and including, in one vignette, a group of citizen-soldiers surrounding and mocking a priest on horseback. In *Charges and Décharges*, one vignette depicts a medieval lady in a tall hennin kneeling outside a confessional booth, where the devil-cleric within has lifted his robe, the better to stroke, and stoke, his impressive erection. You might say that *Souvenirs Patriotiques* and *Charges et Décharges* are two sides of the same coin.

From one angle, Lepoittevin's exuberant scenes of erotic mayhem are without question gross in the extreme. There are human-scale anthropomorphic male genitals engaged in various activities; scatological displays; exposed vaginas aplenty; and everywhere phenomenally huge phalluses, either attached to a demon or standing on their own in assorted situations. The fact that these grotesque anatomies inhabit an imaginary realm is, of course, paramount. Few of us (presumably) would wish to meet a real walking six-foot erect penis with gigantic hairy balls, stumpy legs, and a reptilian tail. Planters' human-size Mr. Peanut is freaky enough; Mr. Penis crosses a line. But that's intrinsic to the transgressive, carnivalesque spirit that runs through and buoys up *Charges et Décharges*, which is all about crossing into forbidden territory: a world of erotic excess in which the body's carnal impulses, needs, desires, and pleasures reign supreme.

Appropriately, there are plenty of attacks (charges) and mighty discharges, or volleys (décharges) throughout Lepoittevin's depictions of diabolical romps. The first leaf of the album sets the tone with a caped devil sporting a prodigious erection that shoots out an orgasmic cannonade of disembodied male and female genitals, along with a woman enjoying a dildo and two tiny airborne couples copulating as best they can. A couple of the penises have wings, and one of the vaginas sports a set of frog-like limbs. In another vignette, women steal large, erect penises from the basket of a peddler preoccupied with licking his own enormous (need it be said) erection as if it were a lollipop; in yet another, a devil-vendor has set out a table of assorted penises (or dildos; it's a little hard to tell) for a pair of eager women deliberating which one to choose.

There is a handful of scenes displaying aggressive demonic attacks on bound (but not apparently distressed) female victims, targeting their vaginas with penile arrows or battering rams. The most serious violence, however, is wrought upon a young moustachioed fellow just on the verge of penetrating his lover, doggy style, as a demon with a raised hatchet suddenly pops up, about to deliver a damaging blow. The caption, "Quel plaisir!" lends just a note of ambiguity. Which one is having fun? In one of the more gleefully perverse concoctions, visibly aroused (well, they invariably are, hardly a need to keep stating it) pint-size devils dive from a shoreline rock straight into the vagina of a woman upended in the water. There are a few pornographic standards: a demon screwing a goat, another performing cunnilingus on a woman while she exhorts him to go easy at it. But how to characterize one of the most impish scenes of all? In "Le Bien et le mal," several devils, the leader waving his hat, dance gleefully out of a cave-like vagina, as if just stepping on (or off) stage.

Quite often, though, the women enthusiastically take charge. They play tug-of-war with one devil, pulling on his (enormously erect, of course) cock while he clutches a tree branch for balance and urges them to keep a firm grip. Another lass chases a flying penis with a butterfly net. Elsewhere a flurry of ladies, most of them nude except for their stockings, eagerly strive to catch a phallic trophy or two from the loaded basket that several demons are tipping over from a window above. Women rub their bottoms against a monumental penile megalith, coo over a pair of cocks merrily dancing to the tune of a piper, or worship a phallus standing tall on an altar. Then there is the young servant girl straining under the weight of the mammoth cock and balls that she has found somewhere and hauled home on her back like a sack of laundry. What she might do with it is a bit of a conundrum. In one of the most elaborate conceits, there is a funeral for a set of jumbo private parts, dead, presumably, of exhaustion; crowned with a wreath and a medal of honor, it is borne on a litter and trailed by a line of weeping women, with a few nuns, too, in the far background. Needless to say, it is a Satanic ritual.

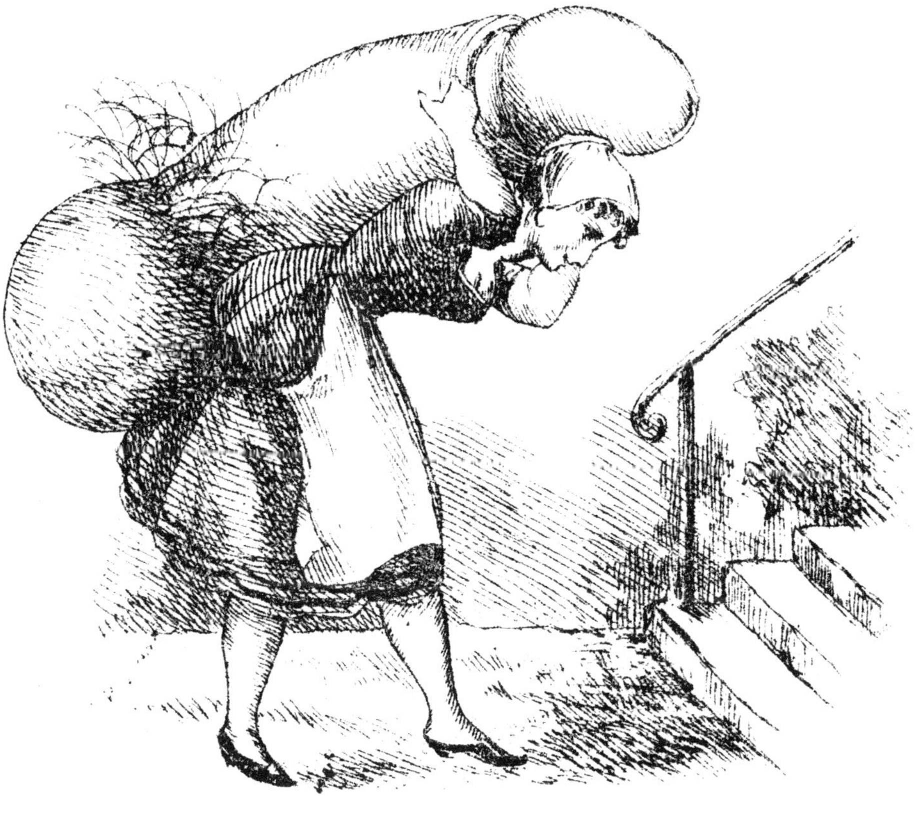

Une trouvaille

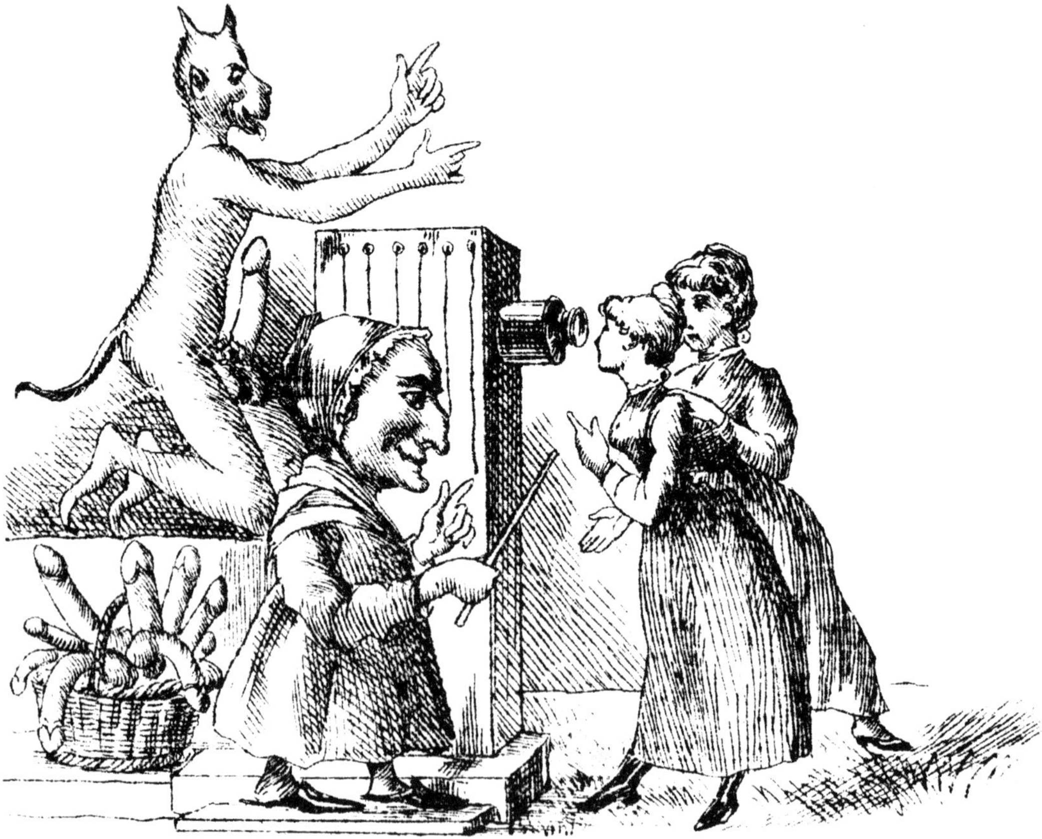

La pièce curieuse

Gargantuan detached penises and testicles are one thing, but the anthropomorphic and very much alive male sexual organs that also populate Lepoittevin's plates are quite another. Their hefty, hairy balls evoke the puffy trunk hose once worn by men of the Tudor era, and, except for one, their glans-penis heads are featureless bulbs without ears, eyes, nose, or mouth. But the penis-men somehow manage to exhibit personality despite that. One, wearing a jacket, is fishing and has just gotten a bite. Not surprisingly, he has caught a tiny penile fish. Another is in a hunting outfit, aiming his rifle at a flying penis that has a vagina under each wing for good measure. There are penises learning to swim, another with chicken legs, and yet another, in eighteenth-century dress, sweeping off his plumed hat as he salutes a startled girl. My favorite, though, is the ballsy fellow by an elegant fireside, comfortably relaxed in an armchair and managing somehow to read *Le Figaro*.

In the early 1830s, Lepoittevin capitalized on the popularity of his diableries, producing six albums in all and inspiring imitators as well. (Indeed, judging by comparison with the original 1830 edition, the images reproduced here could be the work of an ambitious knock-off artist who, while lacking Lepoittevin's technical sophistication, was competent enough to replicate each scene in all its salacious detail.) Once government censors cracked down on obscene ephemera in 1845, though, diableries went much further underground, even, than before. Often the albums were broken up for sale as single sheets, and very few intact copies survived.

In one famous legal case, however, Lepoittevin's diableries were among the star exhibits. In 1951, famed sex researcher Alfred Kinsey ordered a large number of erotic and pornographic books, prints, and photographs from Europe for the research library of the institute that now bears his name. Kinsey intended this booty to serve as bait for U.S. Customs Bureau inspectors, and sure enough, they pounced on the illicit shipment when it arrived in New York on August 2. The subsequent federal court case, *United States vs. 31 Photographs*, ultimately decided in the defendant's favor, and the materials, including Lepoittevin's *Charges et Décharges diaboliques*, were handed over to the Institute in 1958. The court concluded that as long as dirty books and pictures remained in the hands of scientific researchers, they could no longer appeal to prurient interests and were therefore not obscene—as long as no one was allowed to see them unless equipped with the proper credentials. To this day, the Kinsey Institute keeps a low profile and permits access to its collections, for the most part, to serious researchers.

Regardless, the genie has gotten out of the bottle, and prurient interests, for better or worse, are at liberty to roam the Internet for whatever will satisfy their cravings. Even in these jaded times, though, Lepoittevin's devilishly cocky fantasies still seem fresh. Perhaps that's because the artist, with his light touch, didn't take himself, or his themes, too seriously. Wildly inventive and humorously perverse—or perversely humorous—they are at least as likely to tickle the funny bone as to induce a boner.

*

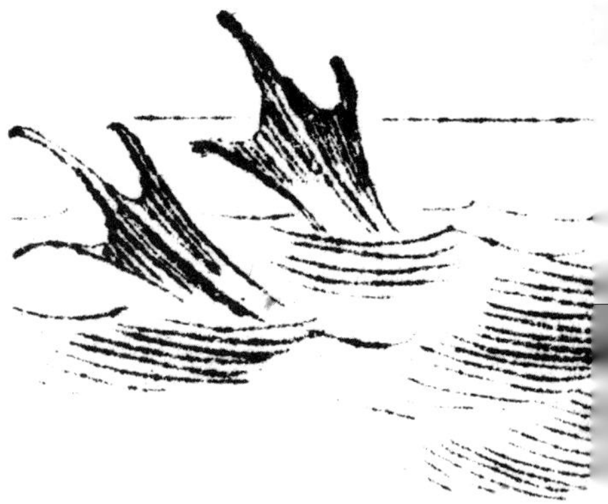

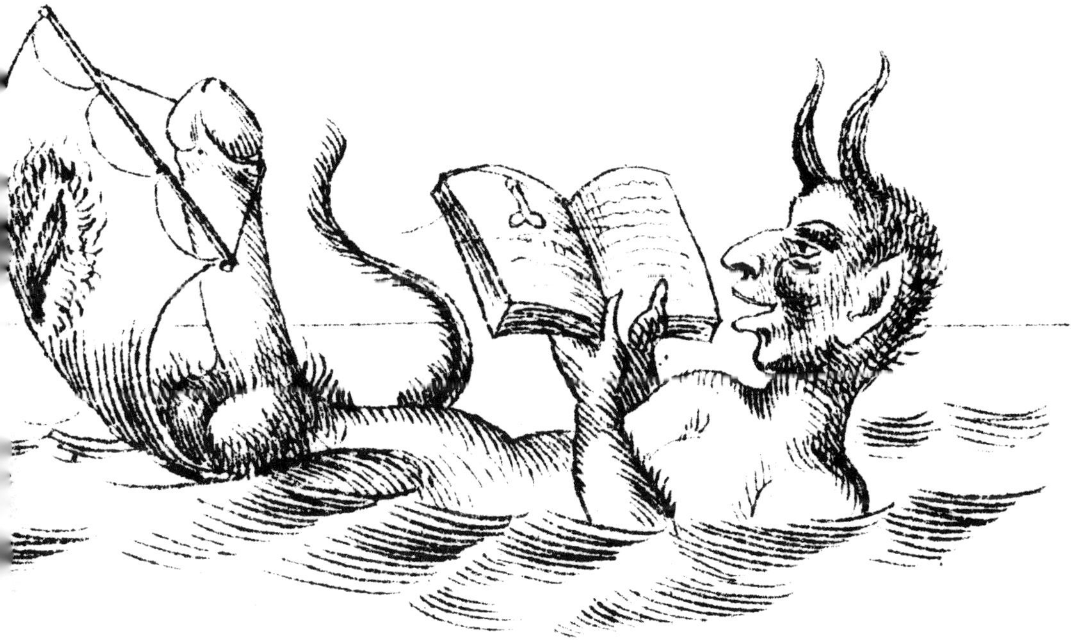

Le premier Naviteur.

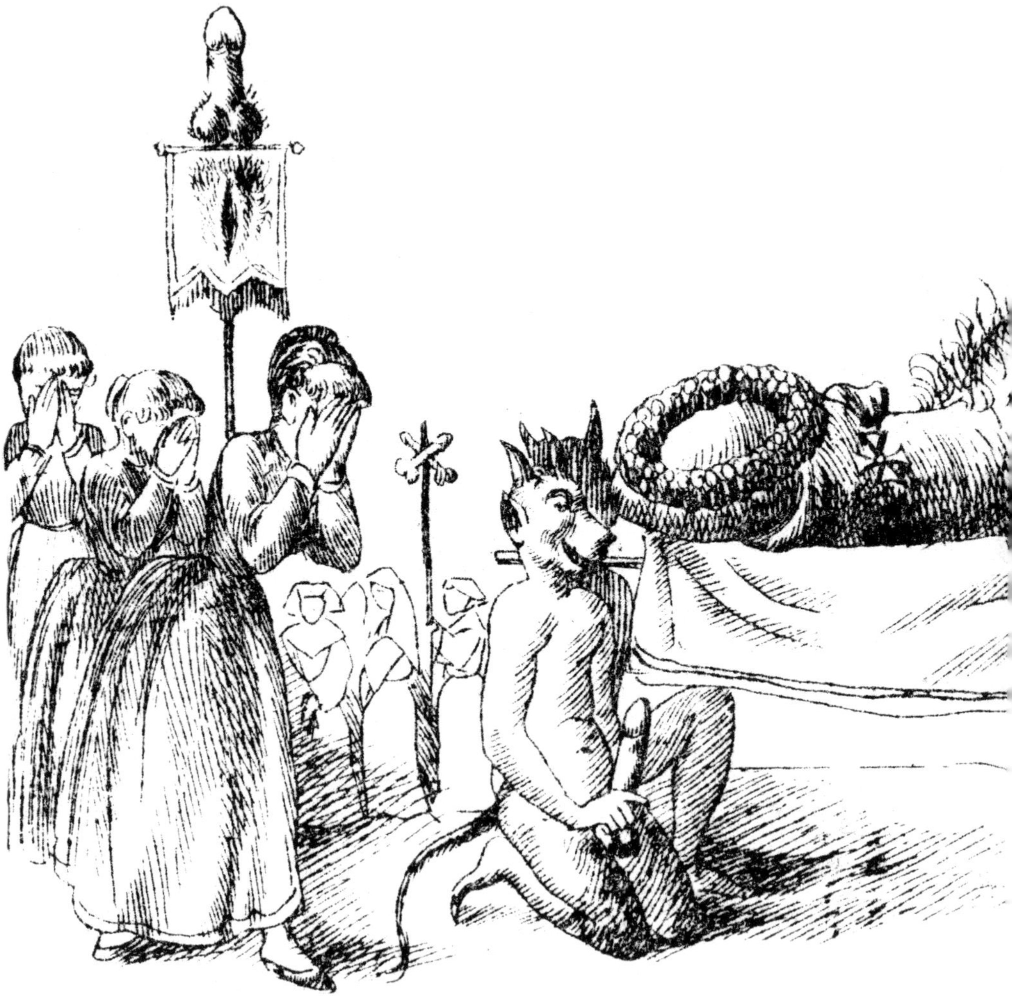

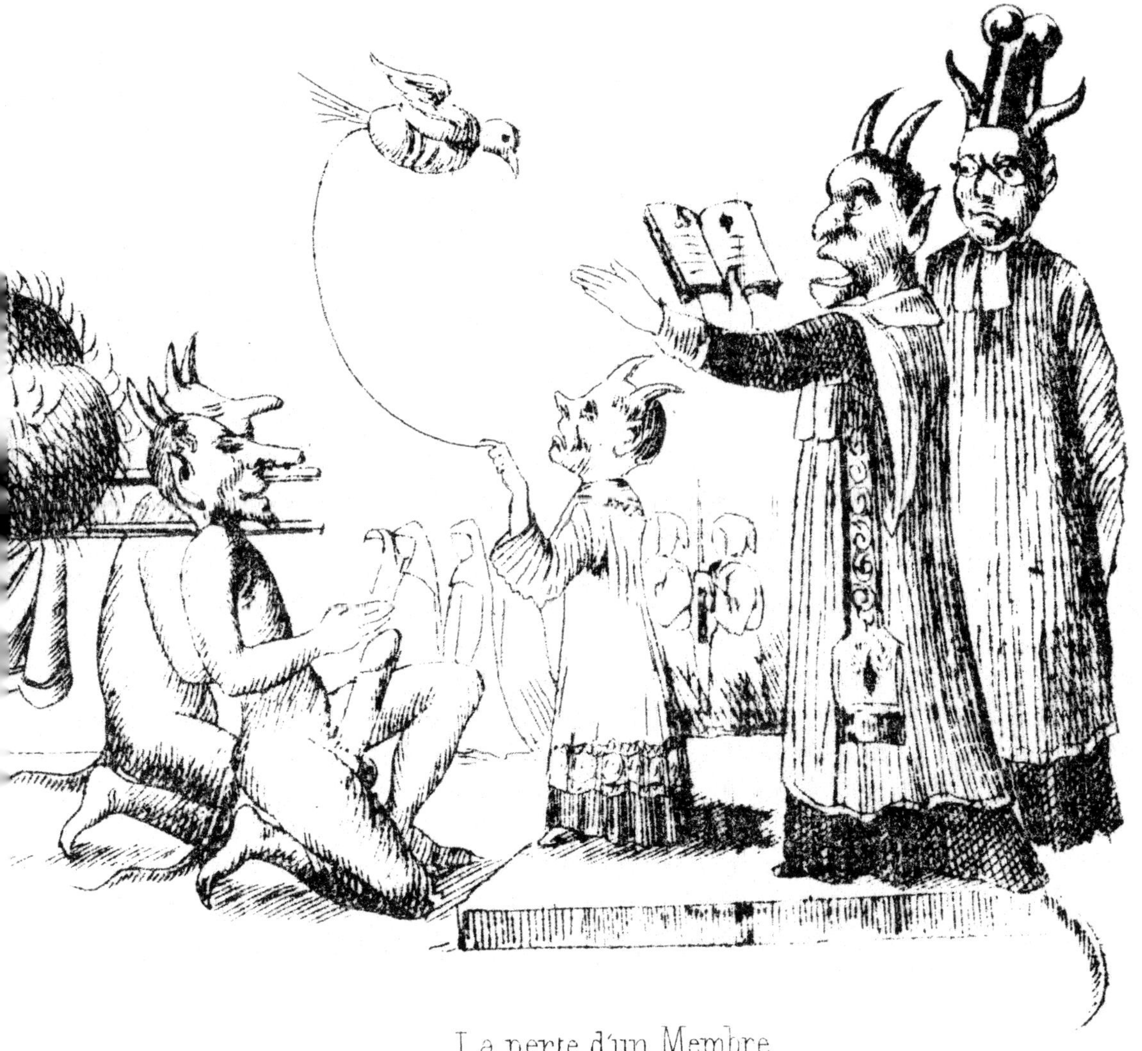

La perte d'un Membre

Cuckold!

A countryman and his wife travelling met some witches on the road. The witch, thinking to put a joke on those straggling persons, said to the gentleman, “I can tell you your fortune. Give me your hand.”

He did so. Having examined it a few minutes, “It is not long ago,” she said, “that your wife made you a cuckold.”

The wife hearing her say so said, “The Devil take these witches, they know everything!”

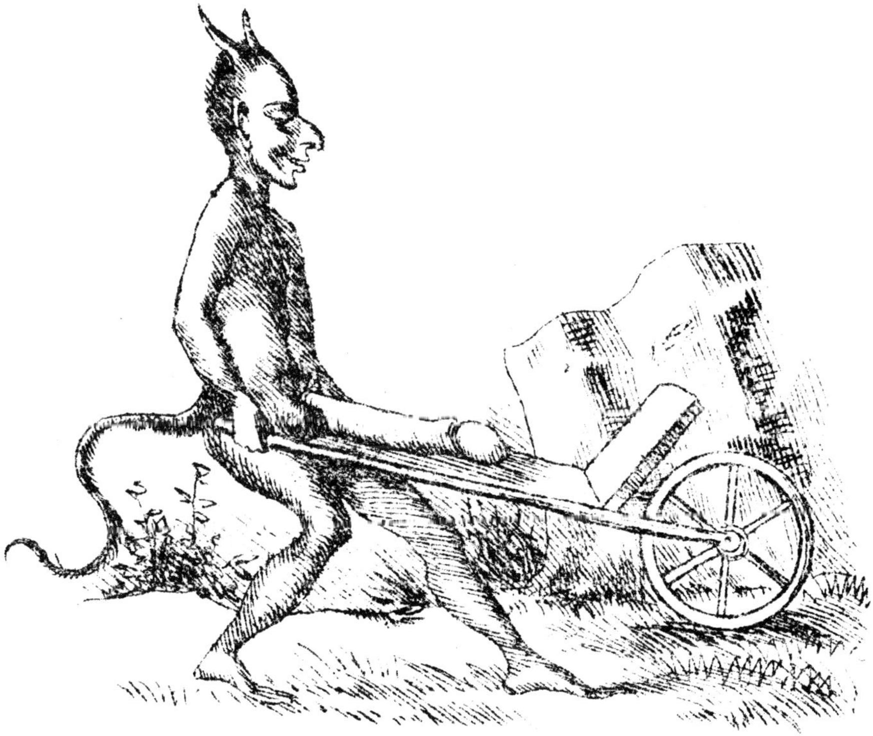

Une grande affaire.

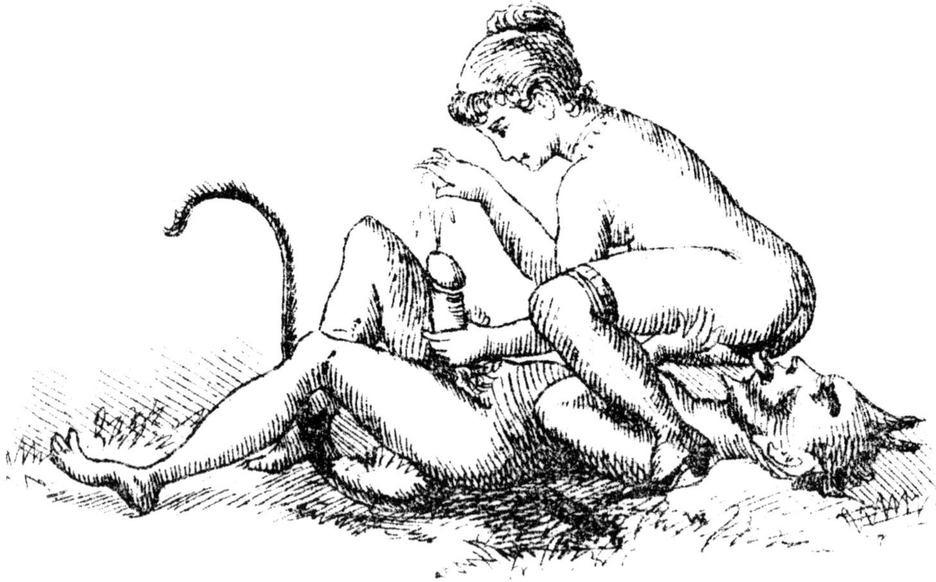

Le Jet d'eau

Ecumenical Accords

A Catholic and a Quaker travelling through a plain where a cross was erected, the Catholic very devoutly bowed to it, which so inflamed the zeal of the honest Quaker, that he told the Catholic with much indignation, "You might as well bow to the gallows, because they are both made of wood."

To which the Catholic replied, "Why, then, in way of salute, may not you as well kiss your wife's ass as well as her mouth, seeing that they are both made of the same material?"

The Family Way

"Mary," said Mrs. Robinson to her servant, "I believe you are in the family way!"

"Yes, ma'am; and so are you!"

"But, girl, you don't understand: I'm married, and have a father for my child."

"Yes, ma'am; and so do I."

"You don't understand; my husband is the father of my child."

"And so he is of mine, ma'am."

"For shame, you hussy; why, my husband wouldn't touch you with a pair of tongs."

"No, ma'am; but he did with his little poker!"

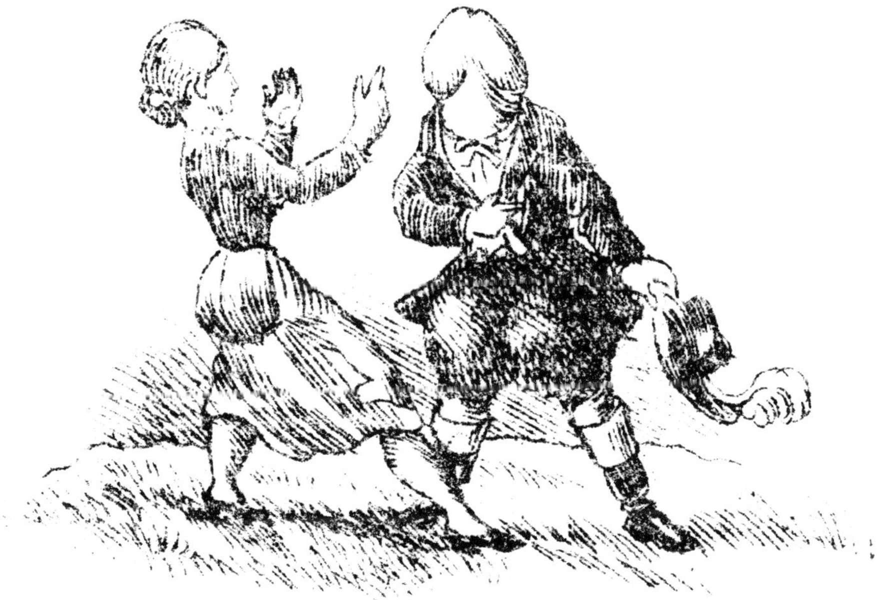

1e Entrevue

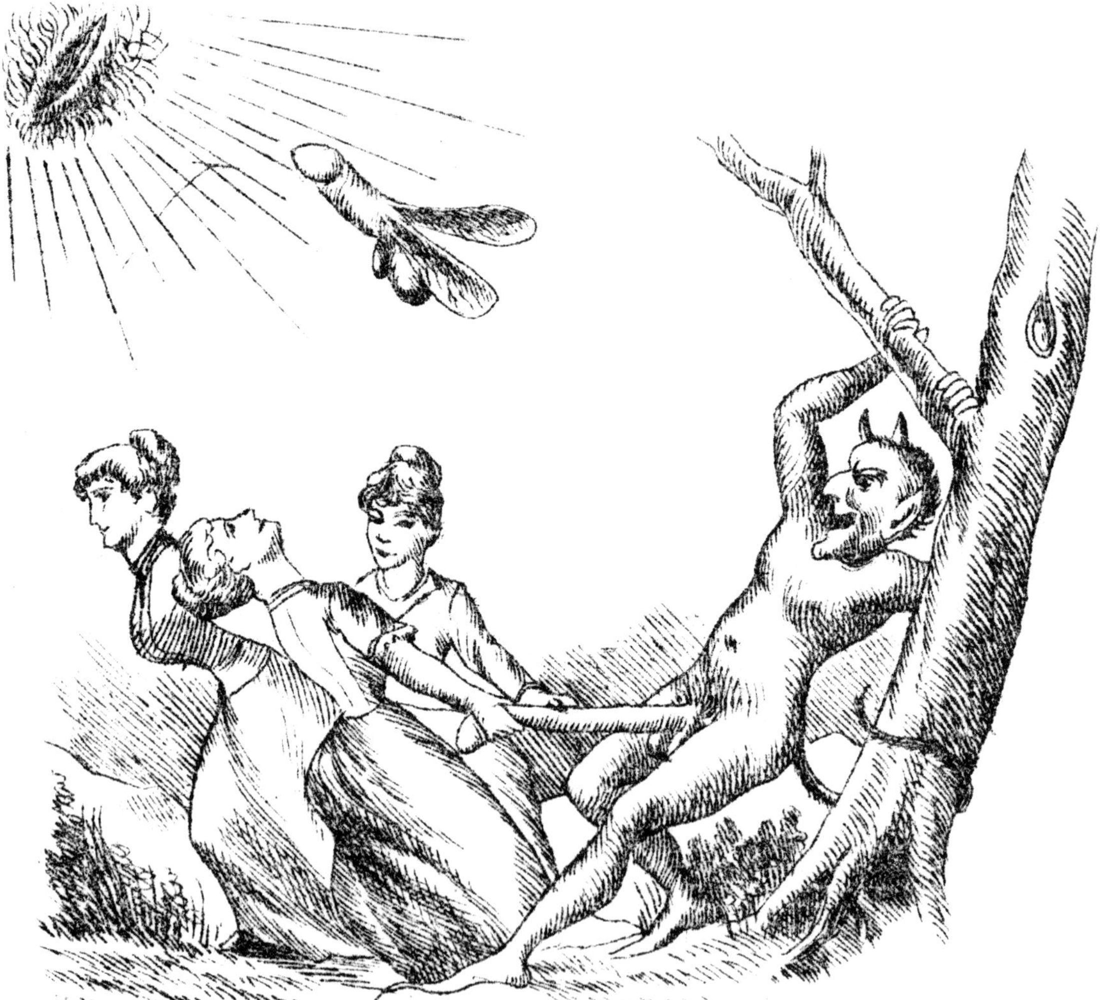

Tiens ferme !

A Growing Concern

A gentleman in the country, who had three daughters, discoursing one evening on rural affairs, and the nature of vegetation, asked one of his daughters what plant or herb she thought grew the fastest?

The young lady replied, asparagus; then he asked the second, who answered, a pompion or gourd. And when the same question was put to the youngest, she replied the pommel of a saddle; which very much surprising the old gentleman, he desired to know what she meant, and how she could make it out?

Why, said she, when I was one day riding behind our John, and the ways being so rough, that I was afraid I should fall off, he cried, "Put your hand about my waist, and lay hold of the pommel of the saddle." And I am sure, papa, when I first took hold of it, it was not much bigger than my ring finger; and in less than a minute, it was thicker than my wrist.

Timbuctoo

Schoolroom during recess. Young lady teacher to boy pupil: "My boy, can you write a verse of four lines, putting in the word Timbuctoo twice and still make sense?"

The boy wrote as follows:

"Tim and I a-hunting went
On the plains of Timbuctoo,
We found three maidens in a tent,
I bucked one and Tim bucked two."

Schoolteacher: "Well, did you get it in twice?"

Boy: "No I did not, but Tim did."

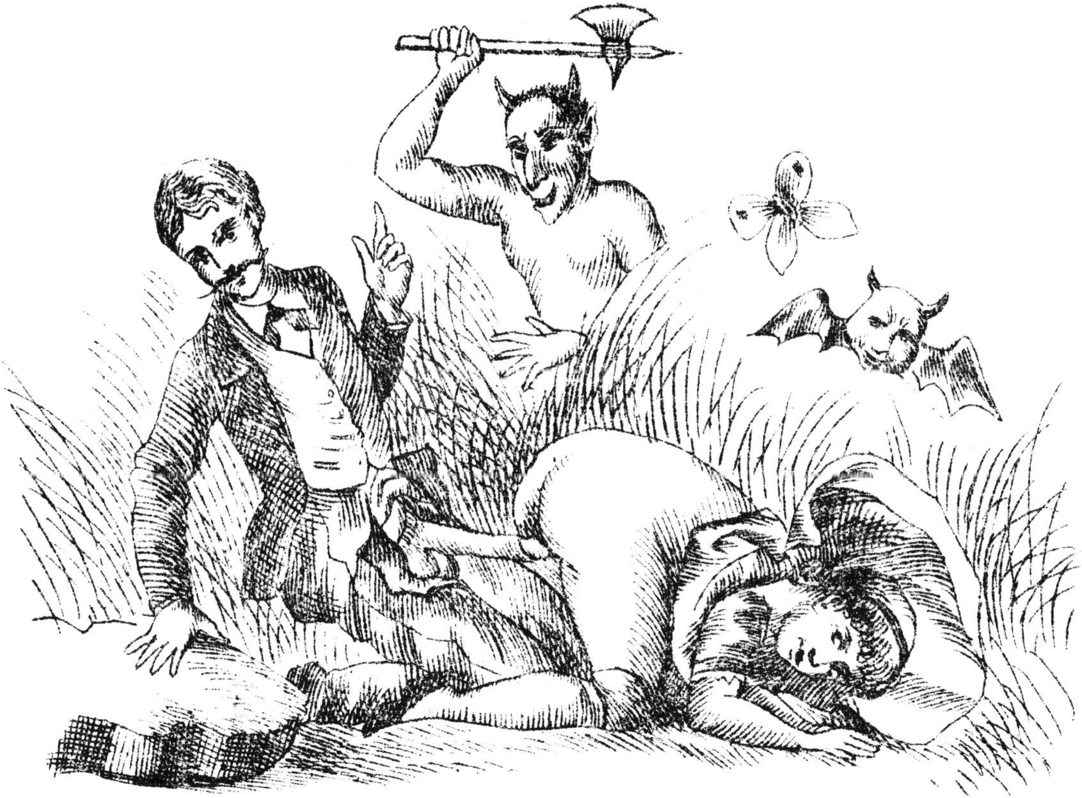

Quel Plaisir!

BON MOTS

A gentleman playing at a romp with a young lady, complained she had given him a confounded prick in his hand.

"I am very sorry for it, said the lady; but if you are resolved to avenge the affront, you may give me a prick in my hand, if you choose it."

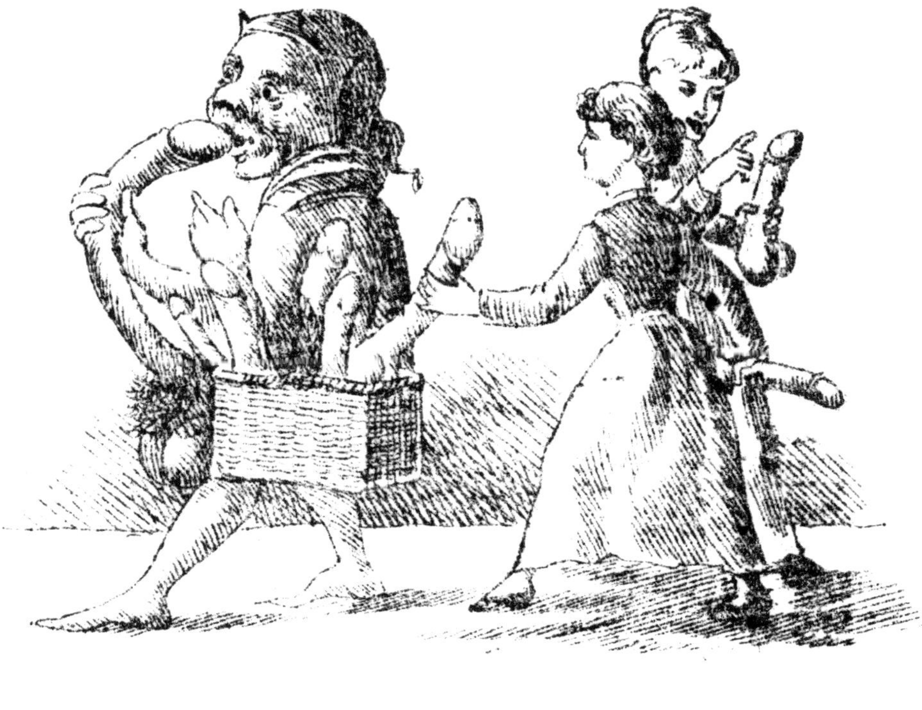

Un vol manie-fesses.

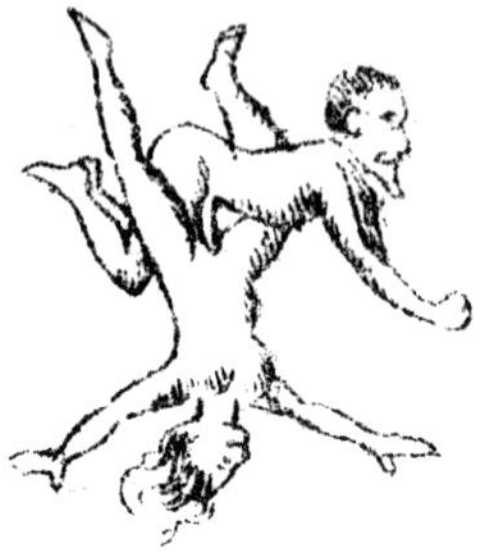

A country farmer going across his grounds in the dusk of the evening, saw a young fellow and a lass very busy near a five-bar gate, in one of his fields, and calling to them to know what they were about.

"No harm, farmer," said the young man, "we are only going to prop-a-gate."

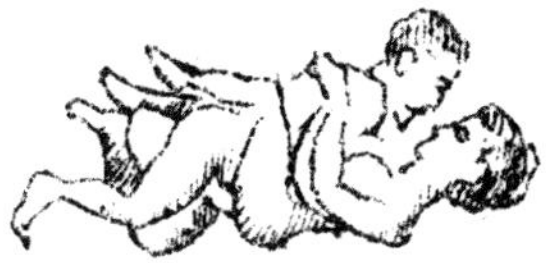

A young spark seeing a pretty girl said, "Sweet heart, give me leave to kiss your hands and feet."

"O lack! Sir," said she, "you are in extremes to aim at both high and low at once; for I have often heard there is virtue in the middle, and there you may kiss—and if you will not you may let it alone."

Lord Wilmot frequently said that he chose travelling on Sundays for two reasons: one, because he had the prayers of the church; and the other, because all the girls he met with had clean linen on.

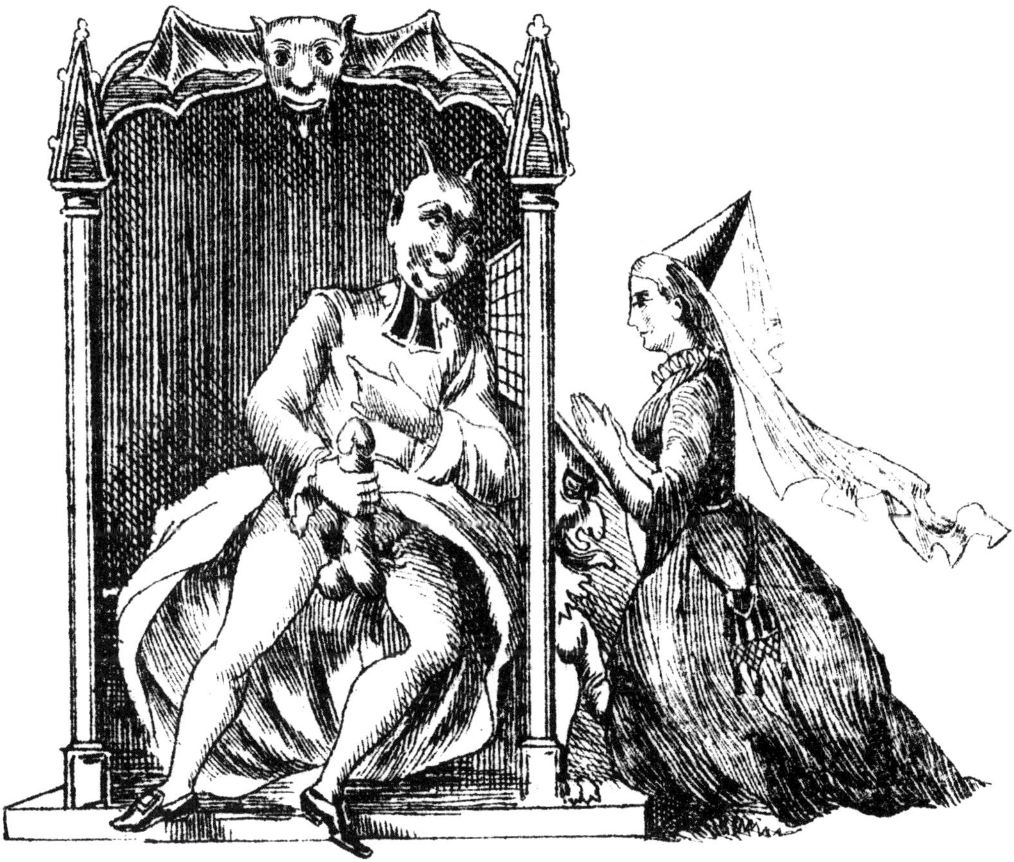

Confiteor

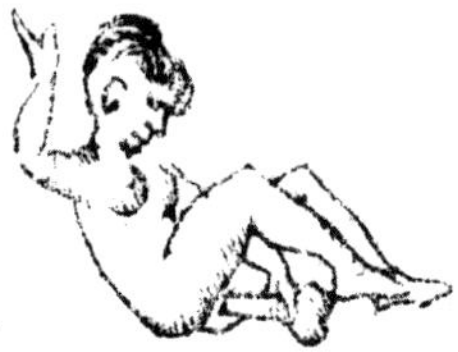

A certain lady, who was very liberal of her favors, declared that she looked upon herself as a queen. "Why so, madam?" says a gentleman then present.

"Because," says she, "there are a great many Members enter my House of Commons."

Biddy, in dusting the statuary, had accidentally broken off the stone penis of a nude figure and was engaged in a futile attempt to glue it on. Her mistress coming in, an explanation followed, and the lady observed that Biddy had turned the pendant upward instead of hanging down as before. So she said: "Why, Biddy, that is not the way it goes. It should hang down."

"Well, ma'am," says Biddy, "all as ever I see stuck up!"

RIDDLES

Why are Patty's breasts like a shrewd adder's tongue?

Where should a lady clap her hands, if a man should enter a room where she was quite naked?

Because they are provoking.

On the man's eyes.

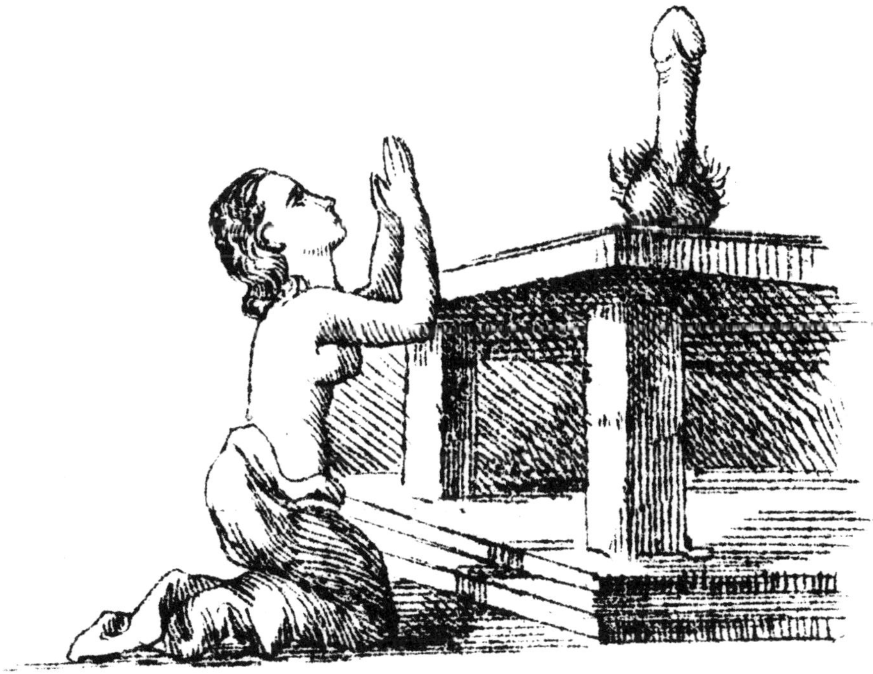

Adoremus.

Why is Fanny like a Sergeant at arms?

I know a lady young and fair,
That has a thing o'er grown with hair;
With which she takes delight in bed,
And dearly loves to have it fed.

What Am I?

Because she takes unruly members into custody.

A lady's lap-dog.

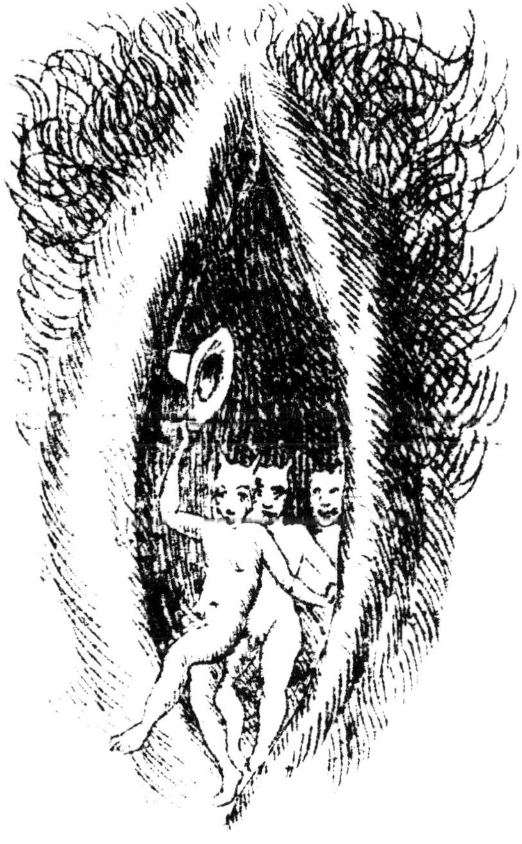

Le Bien et le Mal

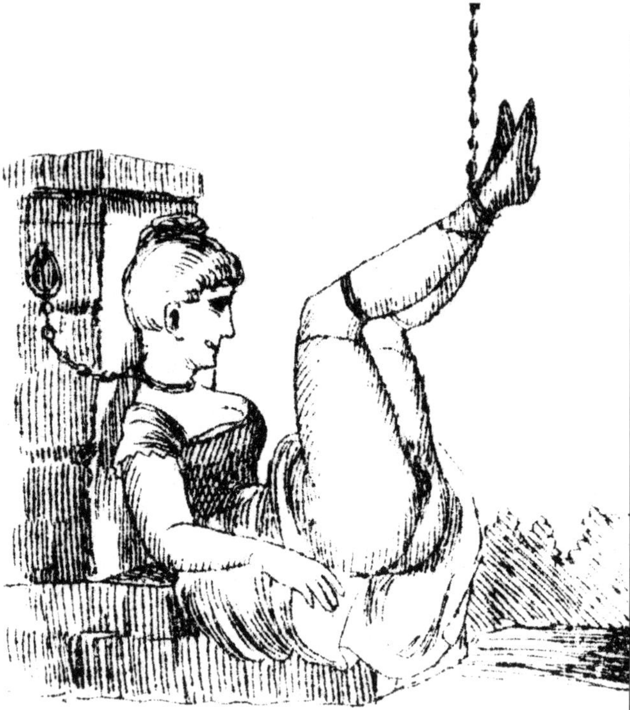

Le Tir agréable

My master often lies
with me,
His wife I oft enjoy;
Yet she's no whore,
nor cuckold he,
And true to both am I.
My clothes nor woman
fit nor man,
They're neither coat
nor gown;
Yet oft both men and
maidens, when
They're naked, have them on.
What's oft my belly, is oft
my back,
And what my feet, my head;
And though I'm up, I have
a knack,
Of being still asleep.

What Am I?

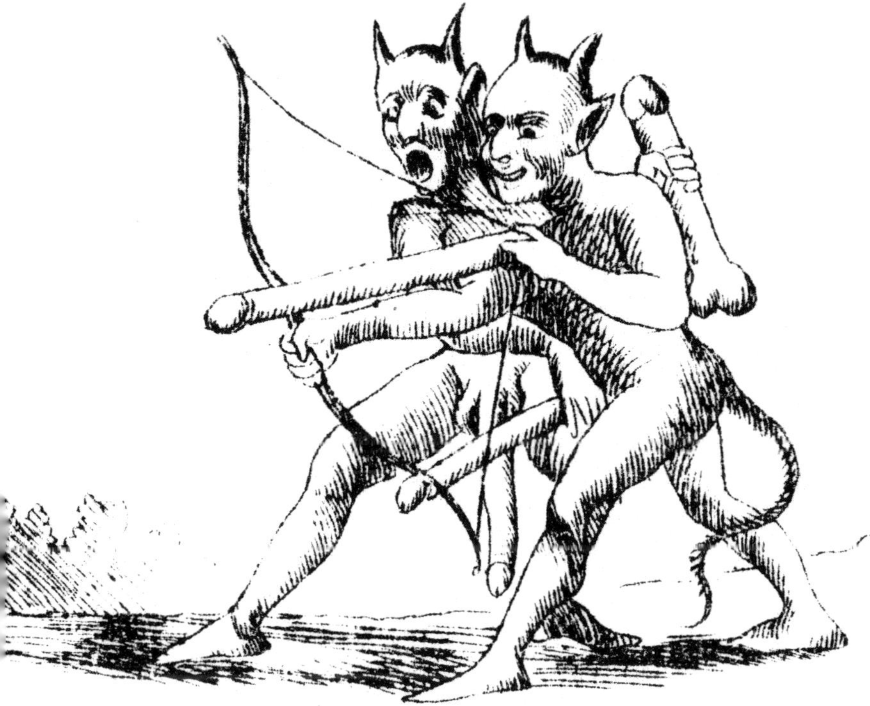

A bed.

LIMERICKS

While his lordship, the peasant girls plied,
His wife didn't linger inside;
The bold gypsy rover
Would get his leg over
And give her a jolly good ride.

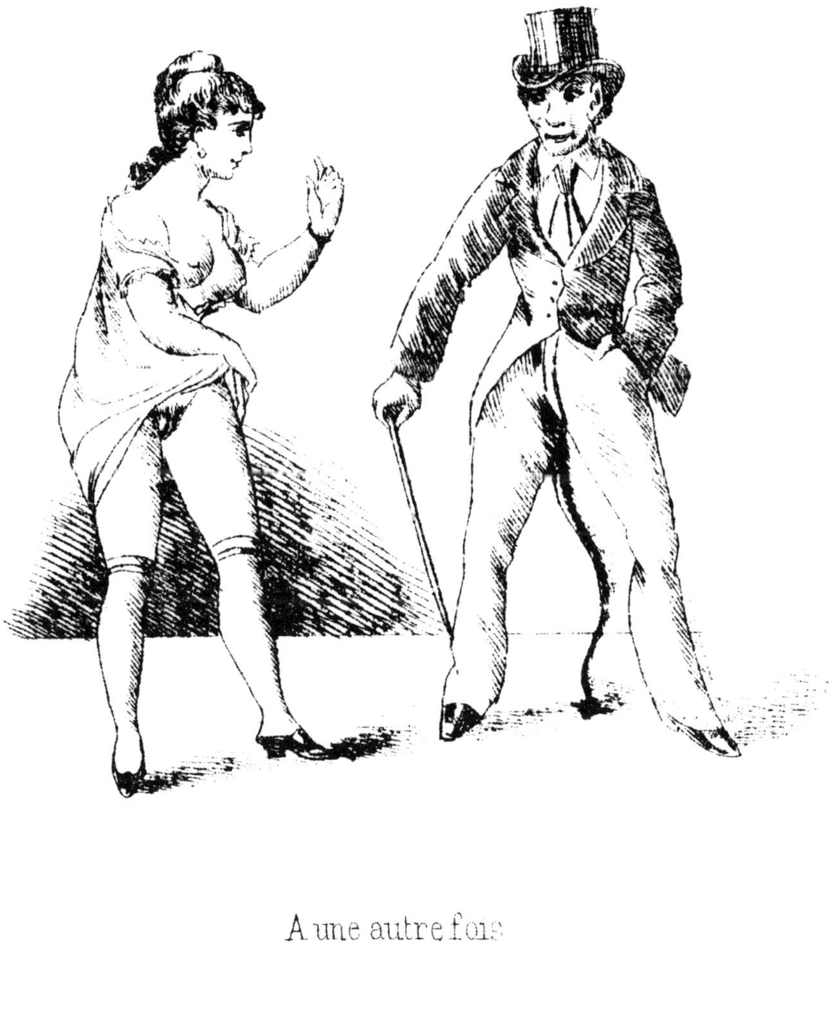

A une autre fois

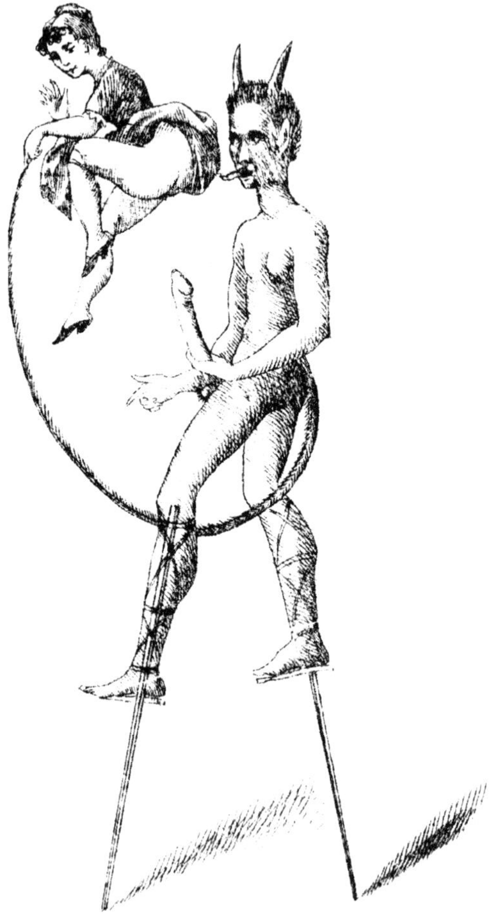

Nouveau Bilboquet avec la manière
de s'en servir

A crusader's wife slipped from the garrison
And had an affair with a Saracen.
She was not over-sexed
Or jealous or vexed,
She just wanted to make a comparison.

—Attributed to Ogden Nash

A once-prudish damsel named Fletcher,
Who succumbed to the wiles of a lecher,
Found it exhilarating
So she kept the guy mating
Till they carried him out on a stretcher!

There was a old lady of Leicester,
And no man had ever caressed her.
And all day she'd wriggle
And giggle and jiggle,
As though seven devils possessed her.

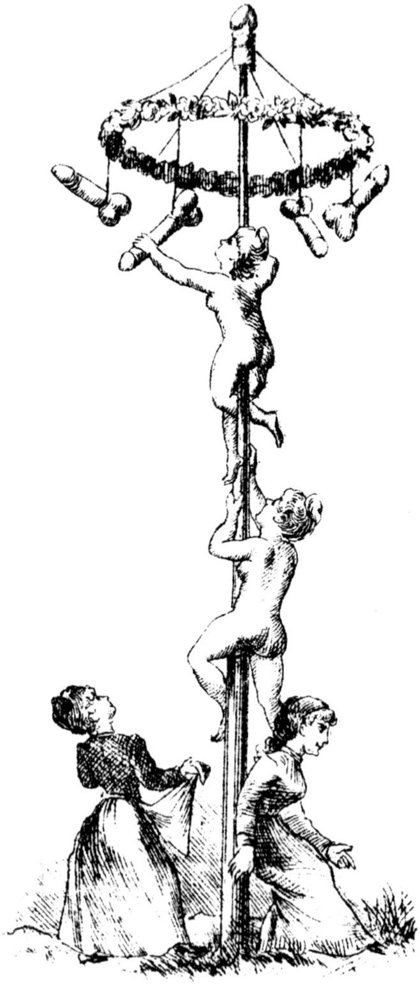

Réjouissance.

The sisters of lust, they will taunt —
Those succubi who will haunt
Your dreams night and day
In every which way,
And do all perversion you want.

"I'm sorry to be such a prig,
But DON'T dine with Satan, that pig.
If you really must munch
On fruit for your lunch —
Reach under my leaf for a fig!"

Now girls, if you find yourself dreamin'
This Satyrday night of a demon
With horns and a tail
Just relax; he's all male
And he'll soon have you pantin' and creamin'.

There was a young lady from Twickinham
Who took every cock without pickin' 'em.
She knelt on the sod
And prayed to her God
To lengthen and strengthen and thicken 'em.

There once was a devil named Mell;
He met a whore he thought was swell.
She hated her pimp;
Mell never went limp.
They married and went straight to hell.

There was a young lady from Glou'ster
Whose parents felt sure they had lost her.
They looked in the grass,
Found the print of her ____
And the knees of the man who had crossed her.

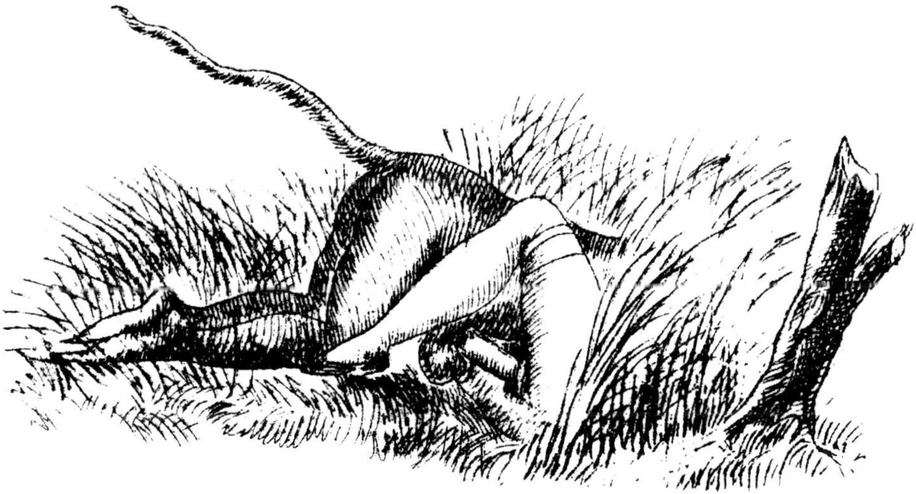

Le pré-o-pinant.

There's a small devil in me tonight;
I'm up, looking for a good fight.
Would you like to tussle
With a little pink muscle?
Come on be my first acolyte.

I thought I'd confess to my priest
How the Devil had made me a beast;
But my sins weren't assuaged,
For I found him engaged
In a wild Bacchanalian feast.

There is a young man in Assizes
Who has testes of two different sizes.
The one is so small
It can't matter at all,
But the other has won several prizes.

There was a young man named McFee
Who was stung in the balls by a bee.
He made oodles of money
By oozing pure honey
Every time he attempted to pee.

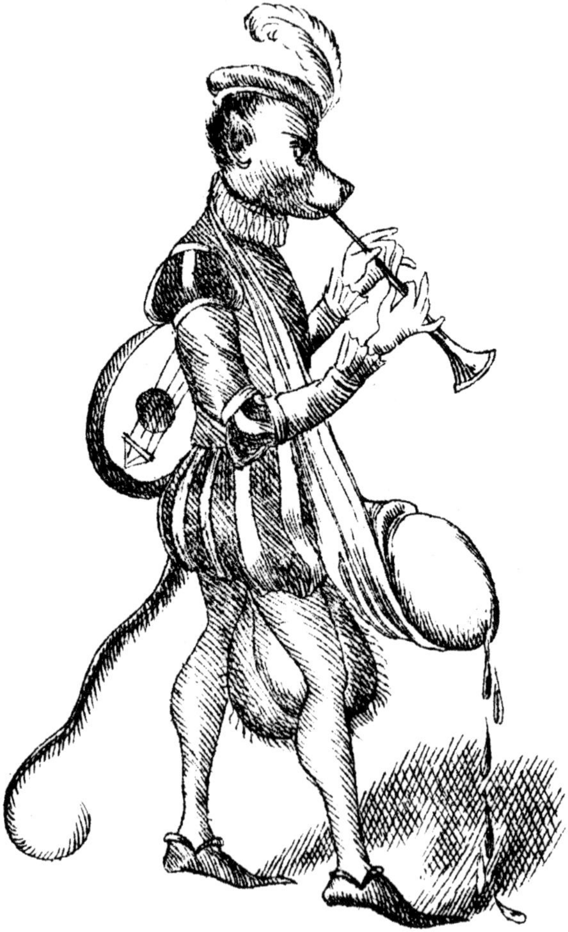

Le Gentil Troubadour

Songs

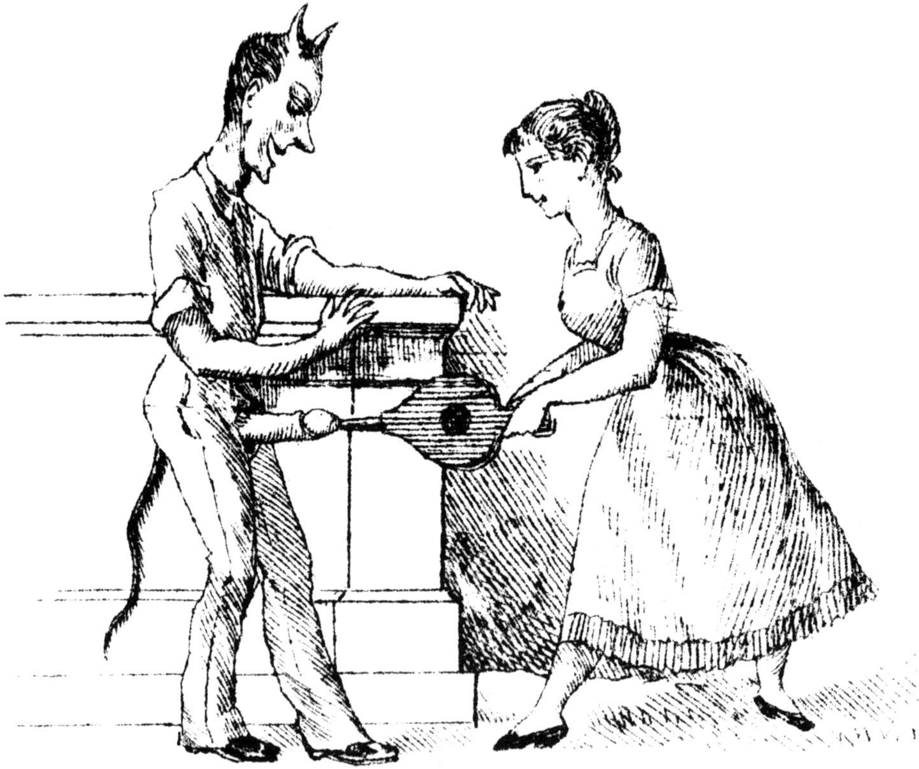

Une Expérience

BETTY'S PANEGYRICK

By Mr. Wm. Turner. (c. 1730)

My Betty is a bonny Lass,
my Betty wears a thumb,
and often looks into a glass,
but 'tis a glass of Rum.

CHORUS:
Bess, Bess, Bess, Betty, Bett,
hasten to my arms,
and then a fig for Kate.

My Betty has a thing below,
But 'tis no matter what,
Can water on a Thing bestow,
But 'tis the Chamber-pott.

{CHORUS}

My Betty has a rowling eye,
And something else that's buff,
Which any one may catch her by,
Tho' it was her black Ruff.

{CHORUS}

My Betty, Crotchets understands,
Also a Fiddle stick, Which,
with mock Ease, her Hand commands,
And eke the longest Prick.

{CHORUS}

She has a penetrating Head,
That understands Proportion,
And if you get her into Bed,
She'll furnish you with Motion.

{CHORUS}

My Betty sings a pleasant song,
All day will you delight,
Especially, if you are long,
She'll please you all the Night.

{CHORUS}

She understands Philosophy,
The Height too, of each Pole,
And, if you get above her Knee,
You may come at her Hole.

{CHORUS}

My Betty has a smirking Look,
And sometimes plays the loose,
And whoe'er peeps into her Book,
Looks like an errant Goose.

{CHORUS}

NINE INCH WILL PLEASE A LADY

By Robert Burns c. 1790s

(Sung to the tune of "The Quaker's Wife")

Come rede me dame, come tell me, dame,
My dame come tell me truly,
What length o' graith, when weel ca'd hame,
Will sair a woman duly?
The carlin clew her wanton tail,
Her wanton tail sae ready -
I learn'd a sang in Annandale,
Nine inch will please a lady.

But for a koontrie cunt like mine,
In sooth, we're nae sae gentle;
We'll take tway thumb-bread to the nine,
And tha's a sonsy pintle;
O leeze me on my Charlie lad,
I'll ne'er forget my Charlie!
Tway roarin handfu's and a daud,
He nidge't it in fu' rarely.

But weary fa' the laithron doup
And may it ne'er ken thrivin!
It's no the length that maks me loup,
But it's the double drivin.-
Come nidge me, Tam, come nidge me Tam,
Come nidge me o'er the nyvel!
Come lowse and lug your battering ram,
And thrash him at my gyvel!

GLOSSARY

rede ~ advise
graith ~ tools
sair ~ serve
carlin ~ old woman
pintle ~ male organ
laithron ~ lazy, inactive
doup ~ backside
gyvel ~ gable

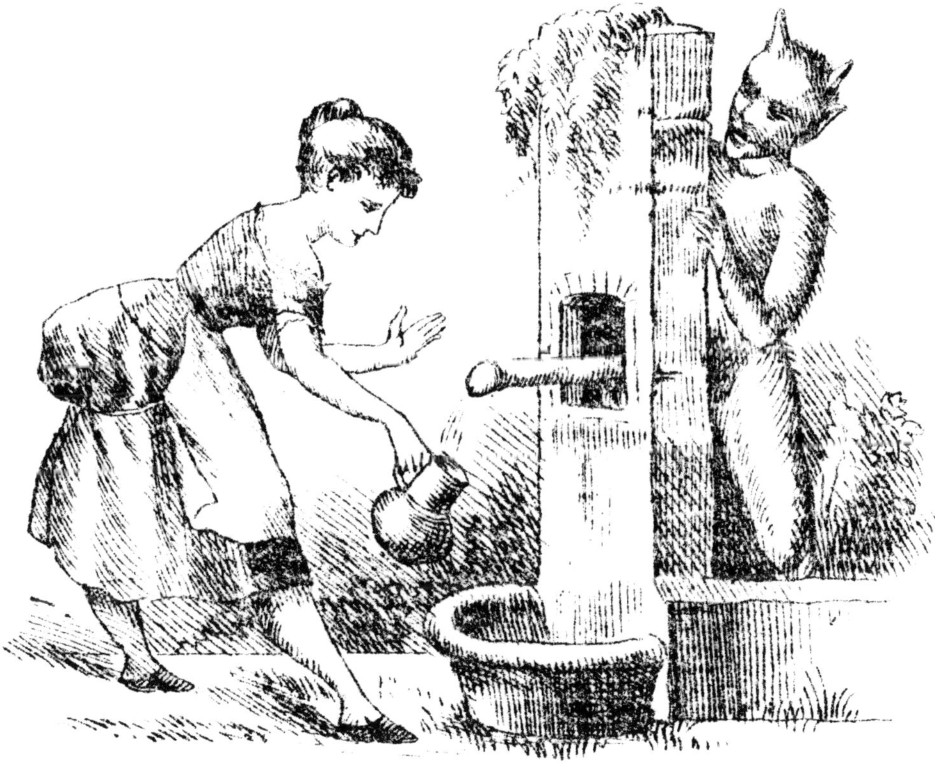

La Fontaine endiablée

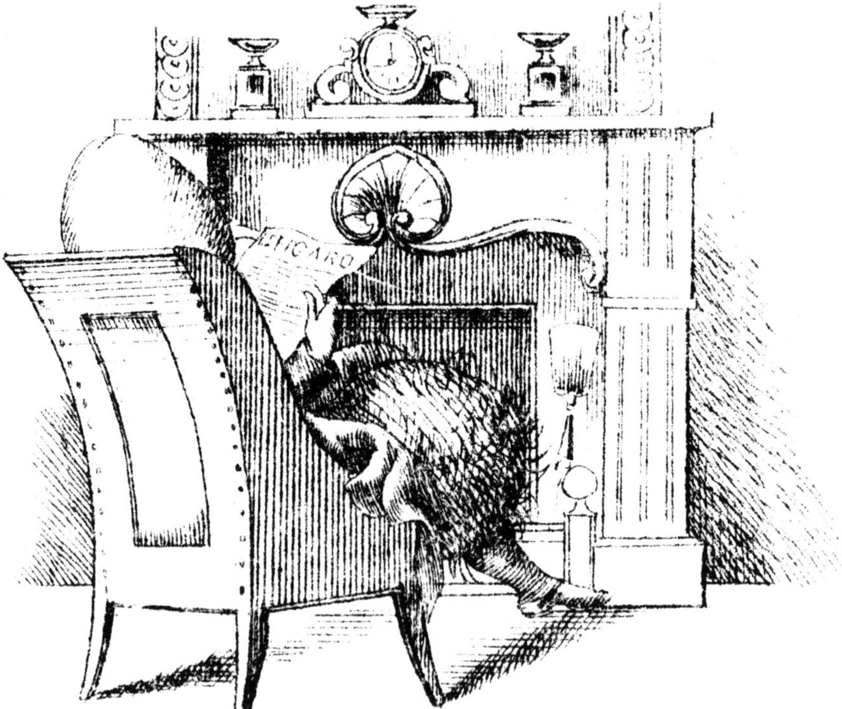

Le Vi-Comte de la Couillardière

Poetry

Cywydd y Gal (Ode to the Penis)

Dafydd ap Gwilym c. 1340

By God penis, you must be guarded
with eye and hand
because of this lawsuit, straight-headed pole,
more carefully than ever now.
Cunt's net-quill, because of complaint
a bridle must be put on your snout
to keep you in check so that you are not indicted
again, take heed [you] despair of minstrels.

To me you are the vilest of rolling pins,
scrotum's horn, do not rise up or wave about,
gift to the noble ladies of Christendom,
nut-pole of the lap's cavity,
snare shape, gander
sleeping in its yearling plumage,
neck with a wet head and milk-giving shaft,
tip of a growing shoot, stop your awkward jerking,
crooked blunt one, accursed pole,
center pillar of a girl's two halves,
head of a stiff conger-eel with a hole in it,

blunt barrier like a fresh hazel-pole.
You are longer than a big man's thigh,
a long night's roaming, chisel of a hundred nights,
auger like a post's shaft,
leather-headed one who is called 'tail'.
You are a crowbar which causes lust,
the bolt of the lid of a girl's bare arse.
There's a tube in your head,
a whistle for fucking every day.
There's an eye in your pate
which finds every woman fair.
Rounded pestle, extending gun,
it is a purgatorial fire for a small cunt,
thatching-stick of girls' laps,
the swift growth is the clapper of a bell,
blunt pod, it dug a family,
snare of skin, nostril with a crop of two testicles.
You are a trouserful of wantonness,
your neck is leather, image of a goose's neckbone,
completely deceitful disposition, pod of lewdness,
door-nail which causes a lawsuit and trouble.

Consider that there is a writ and an indictment,
bow your head, stick for planting children.
It's difficult to keep you under control,
miserable thrust, you are woeful indeed!
Your master is frequently rebuked,
the rottenness through your head is obvious.

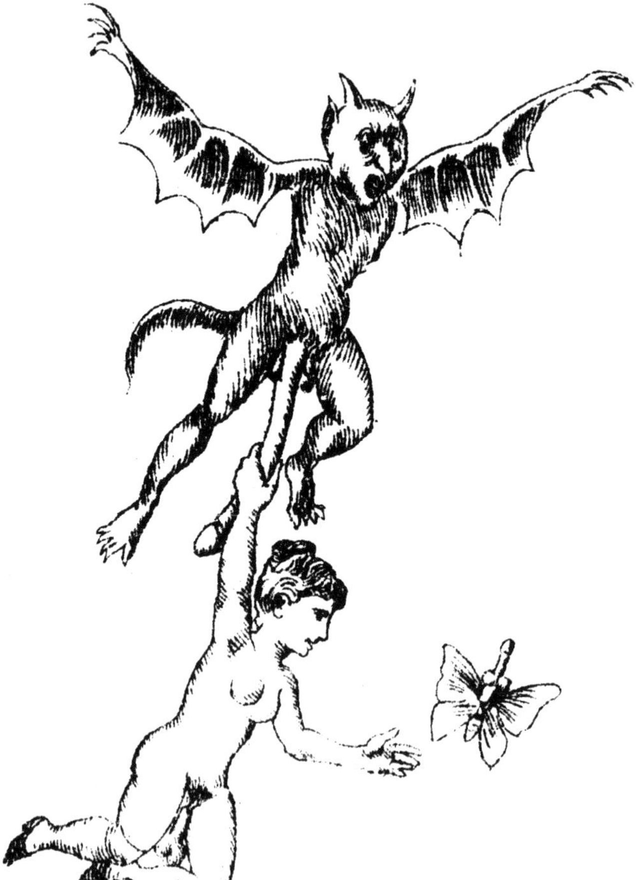

The Hairy Prospect

or the Devil in a Fright

THOMAS ROWLANDSON c. 1799

Once on a time the Sire of evil,
In plainer English call'd the Devil,
Some new experiment to try
At Chloe cast a roguish eye;
But she who all his arts defied,
Pull'd up and shew'd her sexes pride:
A thing all shagg'd about with hair,
So much it made old Satan stare,
Who frightened at the grim display,
Takes to his heels and runs away.

Signior Dildo

John Rochester, 2nd Earl of Wilmot

You ladies of merry England
Who have been to kiss the Duchess's hand,
Pray, did you not lately observe in the show
A noble Italian called Signior Dildo?

This signior was one of the Duchess's train
And helped to conduct her over the main;
But now she cries out, 'To the Duke I will go,
I have no more need for Signior Dildo.'

At the Sign of the Cross in St James's Street,
When next you go thither to make yourselves sweet
By buying of powder, gloves, essence, or so,
You may chance to get a sight of Signior Dildo.

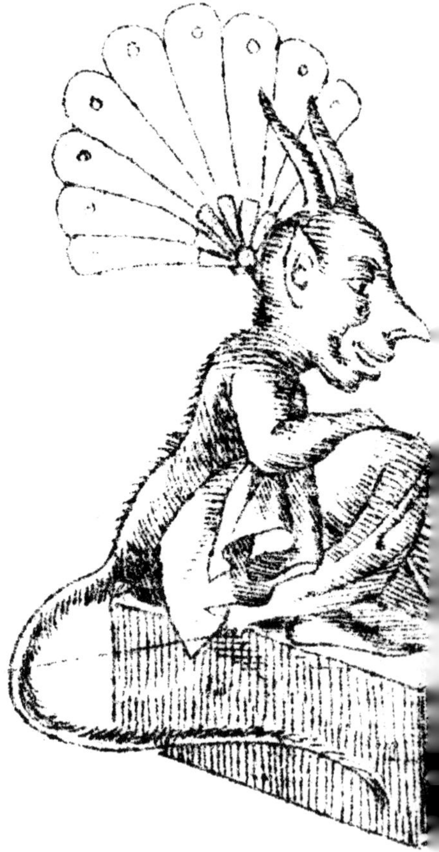

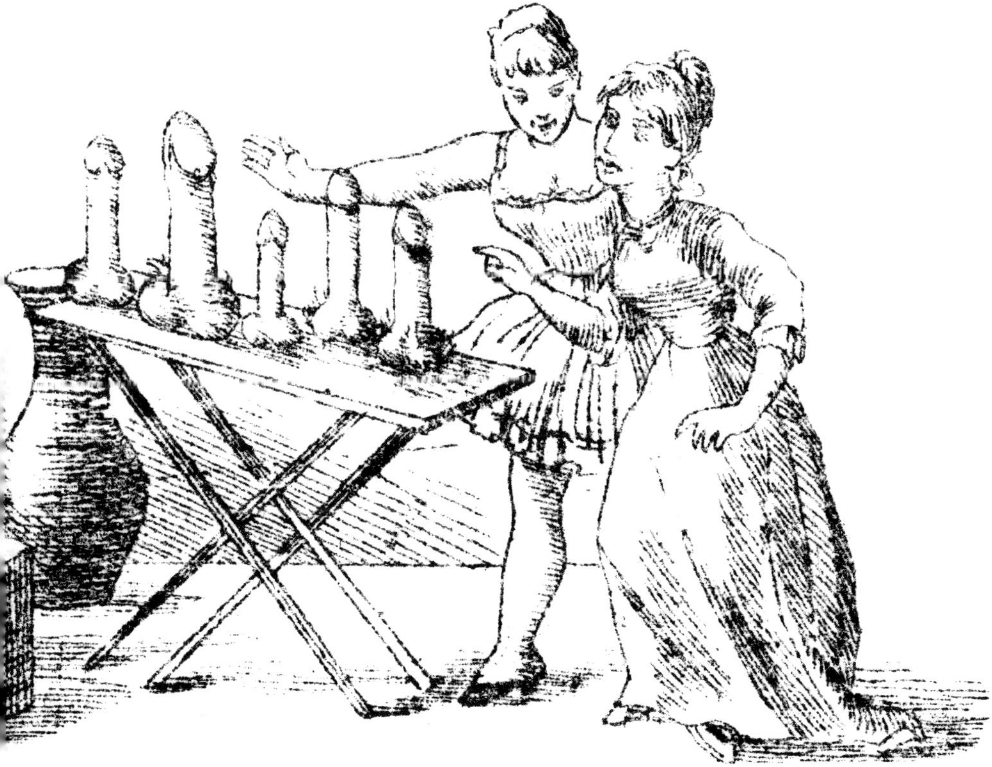

Le Choix dans la Boutique

Signior Dildo

CONTINUED

You would take him at first for no person of note,
Because he appears in a plain leather coat,
But when you his virtuous abilities know,
You'll fall down and worship Signior Dildo.

My Lady Southesk, heaven prosper her for't,
First clothed him in satin, then brought him to court;
But his head in the circle he scarcely durst show,
So modest a youth was Signior Dildo.

The good Lady Suffolk, thinking no harm,
Had got this poor stranger hid under her arm.
Lady Betty by chance came the secret to know
And from her own mother stole Signior Dildo.

The Countess of Falmouth, of whom people tell
Her footmen wear shirts of a guinea an ell,
Might save that expense, if she did but know
How lusty a swinger is Signior Dildo.

By the help of this gallant the Countess of Rafe
Against the fierce Harris preserved herself safe;
She stifled him almost beneath her pillow,
So closely she embraced Signior Dildo.

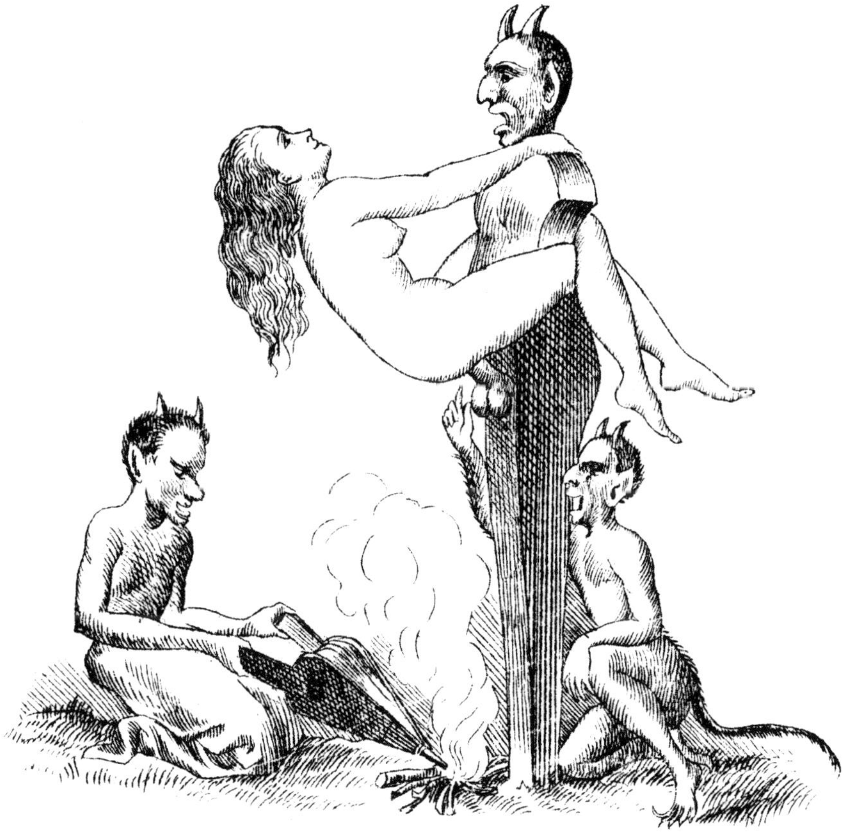

L'heureux Priape

Signior Dildo

CONTINUED

The pattern of virtue, Her Grace of Cleveland,
Has swallowed more pricks than the ocean has sand;
But by rubbing and scrubbing so wide does it grow,
It is fit for just nothing but Signior Dildo.

Our dainty fine duchesses have got a trick
To dote on a fool for the sake of his prick,
The fops were undone did their graces but know
The discretion and vigour of Signior Dildo.

The Duchess of Modena, though she looks so high,
With such a gallant is content to lie,
And for fear that the English her secrets should know,
For her gentleman usher took Signior Dildo.

The Countess o' th' Cockpit (who knows not her name?
She's famous in story for a killing dame),
When all her old lovers forsake her, I trow,
She'll then be contented with Signior Dildo.

Red Howard, Red Sheldon, and Temple so tall
Complain of his absence so long from Whitehall.
Signior Barnard has promised a journey to go
And bring back his countryman, Signior Dildo.

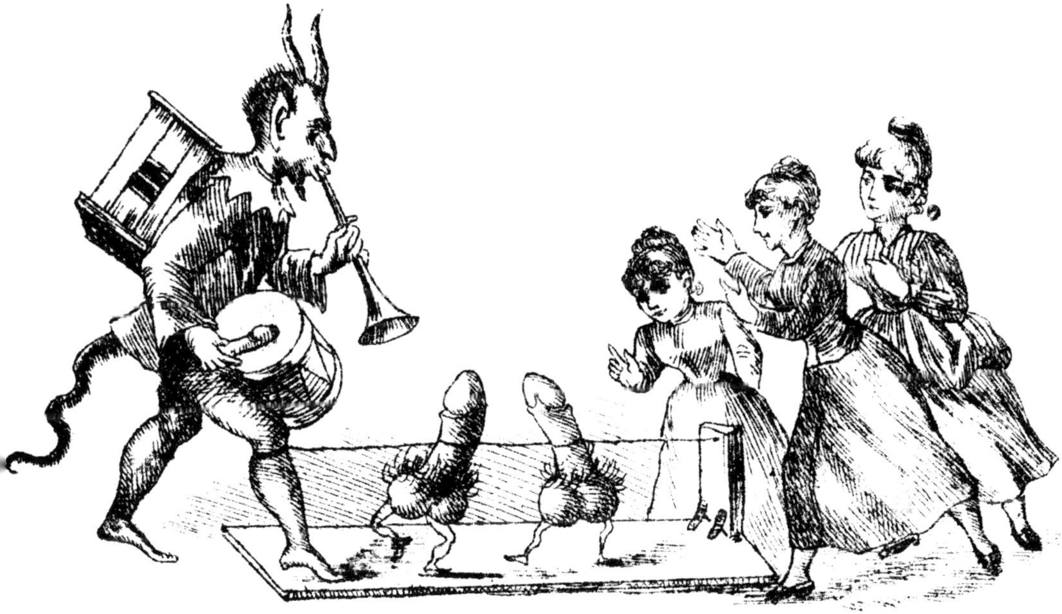

Oh! qu'ils sont gentils.

Signior Dildo

CONTINUED

Doll Howard no longer with His Highness must range,
And therefore is proferred this civil exchange:
Her teeth being rotten, she smells best below,
And needs must be fitted for Signior Dildo.

St Albans with wrinkles and smiles in his face,
Whose kindness to strangers becomes his high place,
In his coach and six horses is gone to Bergo
To take the fresh air with Signior Dildo.

Were this signior but known to the citizen fops,
He'd keep their fine wives from the foremen o' their shops;
But the rascals deserve their horns should still grow
For burning the Pope and his nephew, Dildo.

Tom Killigrew's wife, that Holland fine flower,
At the sight of this signior did fart and belch sour,
And her Dutch breeding the further to show,
Says, 'Welcome to England, Mynheer Van Dildo.'

He civilly came to the Cockpit one night,
And proferred his service to fair Madam Knight.
Quoth she, 'I intrigue with Captain Cazzo;
Your nose in mine arse, good Signior Dildo.'

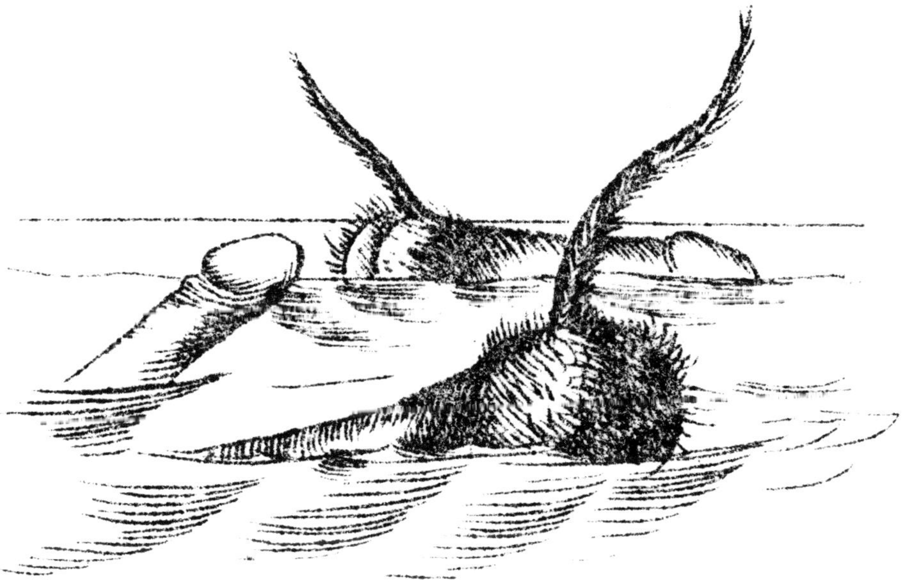

Ecole de Natation

Signior Dildo

CONTINUED

This signior is sound, safe, ready, and dumb
As ever was candle, carrot, or thumb;
Then away with these nasty devices, and show
How you rate the just merit of Signior Dildo.

Count Cazzo, who carries his nose very high,
In passion he swore his rival should die;
Then shut himself up to let the world know
Flesh and blood could not bear it from Signior Dildo.

A rabble of pricks who were welcome before,
Now finding the porter denied them the door,
Maliciously waited his coming below
And inhumanly fell on Signior Dildo.

Nigh wearied out, the poor stranger did fly,
And along the Pall Mall they followed full cry;
The women concerned from every window
Cried, 'For heaven's sake, save Signior Dildo.'

The good Lady Sandys burst into a laughter
To see how the ballocks came wobbling after,
And had not their weight retarded the foe,
Indeed't had gone hard with Signior Dildo.

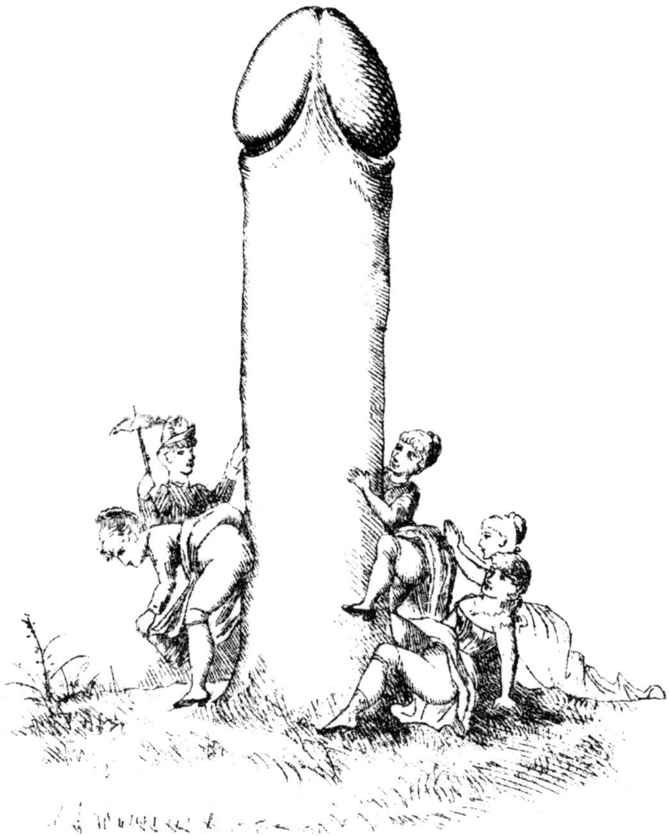

L'Arbre-de-Vie.

Poor Celia

(Author Unknown, English, c. 1820)

Poor Celia slipping, had a fall,
And show'd her naked bum to all,
Which did such beauteous charms display;
It sham'd the lustre of the day,—
I Transported at the sight, I cry'd,
In pity, gentle Celia, hide
The dazzling beams of your backside !
For should it lie uncover'd thus,
All human kind would crave a buss.—
Assist me all ye sacred nine,
To praise a bum that's all divine;
Not all the goddesses on high,
Who reign above the starry sky,

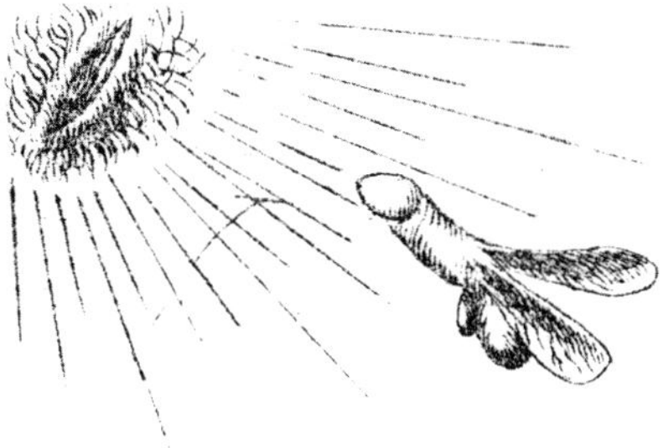

Should they turn up their tails to view,
Can show an arse as fair as you!
The Town Lady to her young Admirer,
Away, young fool! I give all thy flatt'ries o'er
I'm neither saint nor angel, but a whore;
If thou'rt in love, and wounded art by me,
I'll prove thy kind physician for a fee.
If thou hast any fond desire to do't,
Be generous at once, and let's go to't;
Money's alone the god that makes us kind,
For that we give up all you men can find;
For gold we show you all love's pleasing crotchets;
But shut our legs to those that shut their pockets.

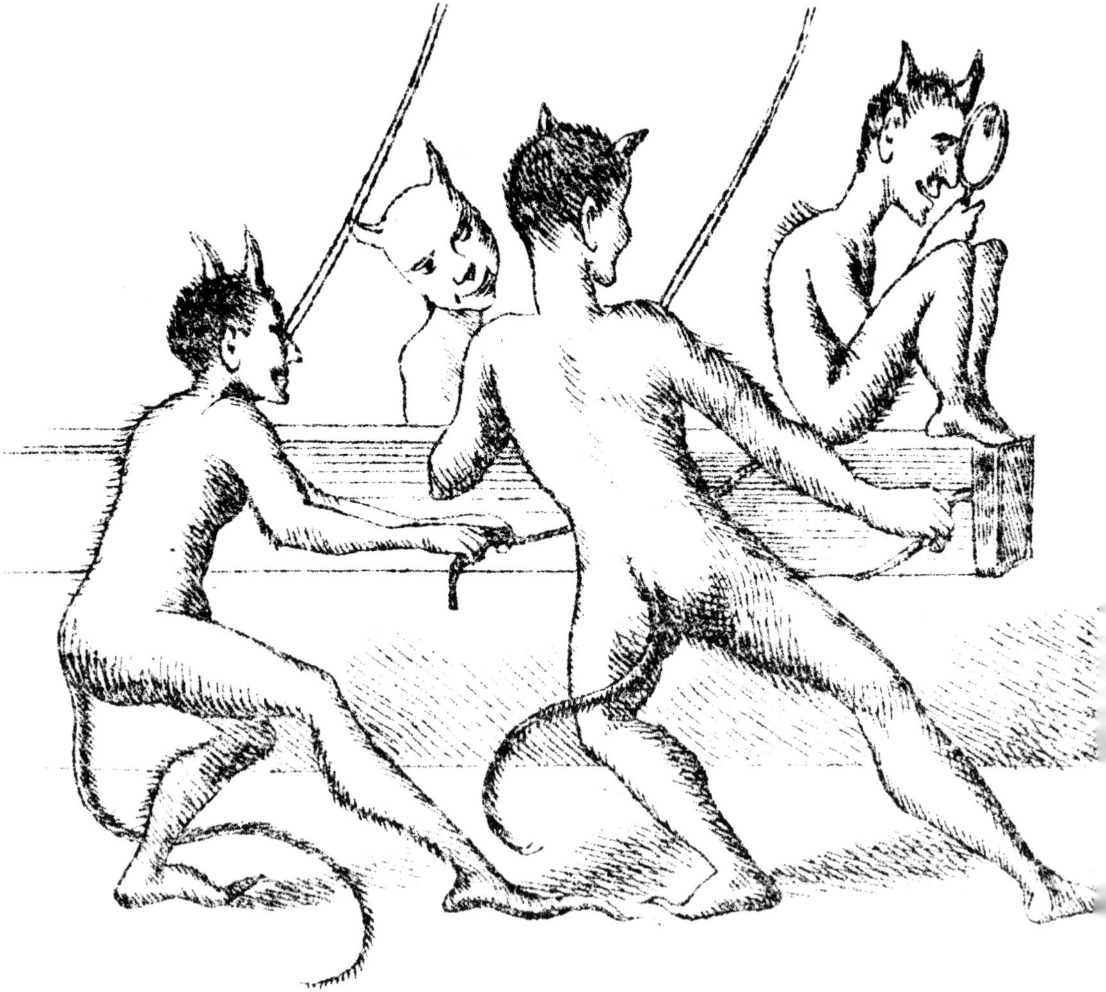

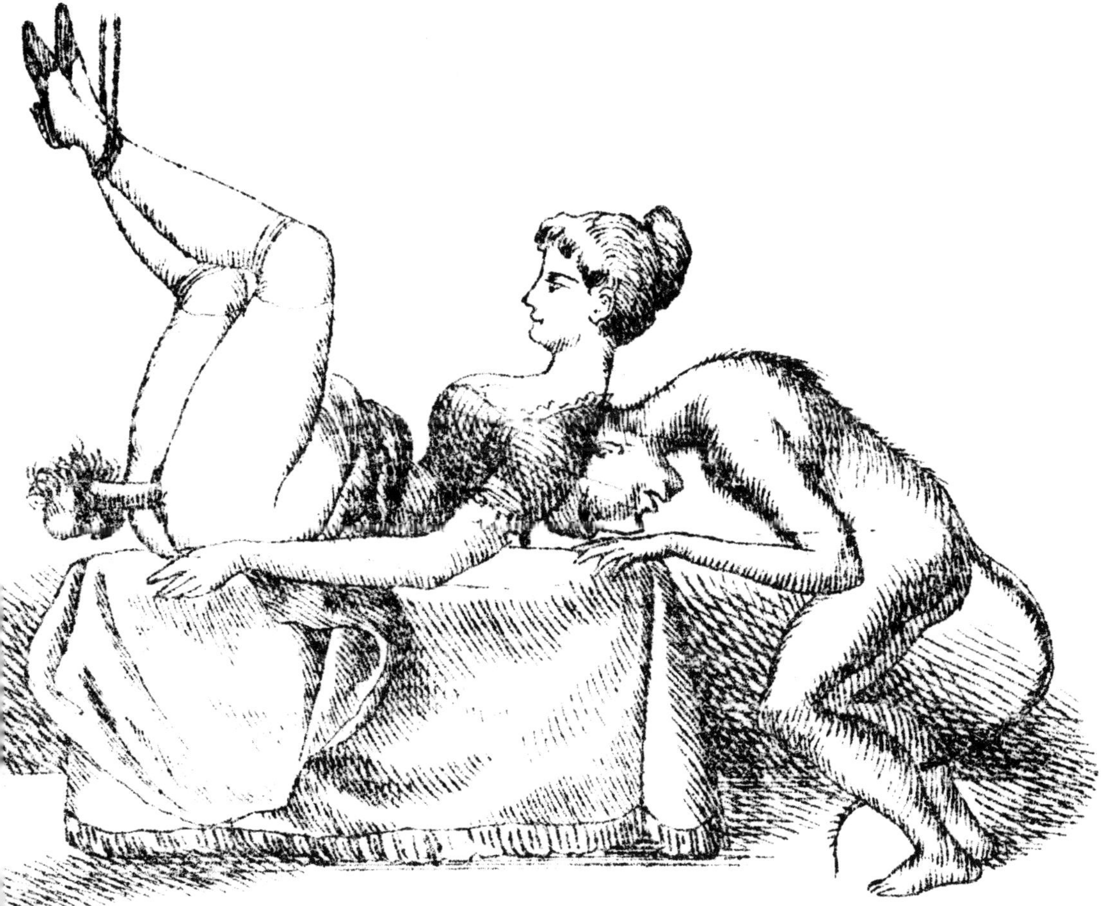

un Pucelage

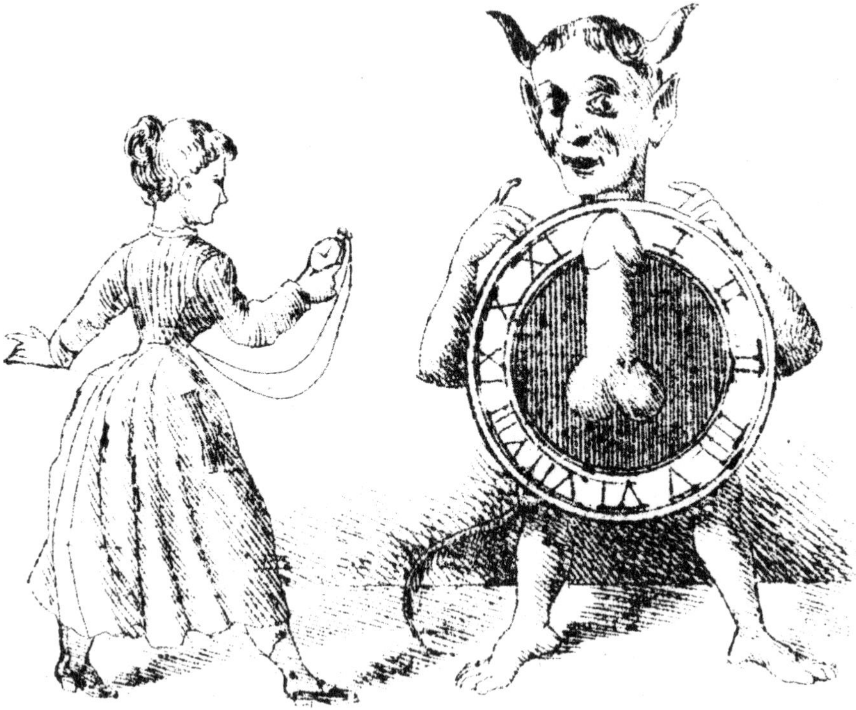

Comme il avance !

Here's to the men!
When I meet 'em, I like 'em,
When I like 'em, I kiss 'em,
When I kiss 'em, I love 'em,
When I love 'em, I let 'em,
When I let 'em, I lose 'em,
God damn 'em!

There was an old man
At Brighton last year
Whose hobby was swimming
Round the government pier.
He dove and he swam
Way out to a rock
And amused all the ladies
By shaking his…
Fist at the copper
Standing on the shore,
The copper who had
Pinched him once before.

They pursued him in small boats
But were unable to pass
For the dirty old rascal
Would then show his…
Wonderful maneuvers
In swimming so fine
His wonderful muscles
Before and behind.

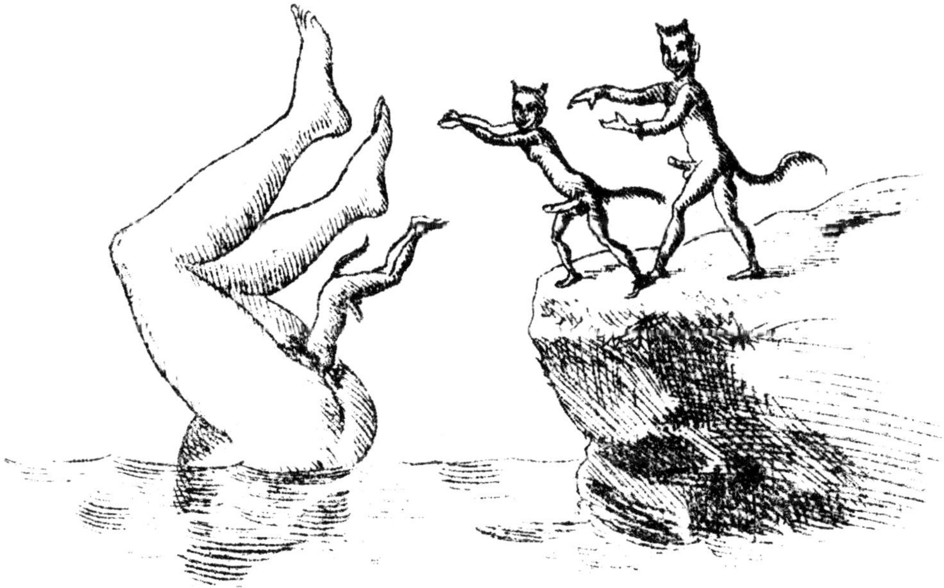

Oh! c'te tête !

Sonnet by Aretino

Embrace me dearest, one quick mad embrace,
Since we created were for love and lust,
And if you revel in the phallic thrust,
I yearn for yonder mossy dell apace.
And were debauchery prizeful after death,
I'd bid the dying make a note of this:
Give Adam and his Eve a taste of bliss,
Since love's sweet fire deprived them of Life's breath.
Yet had these worthies never fallen low,
By eating of the fruit that was denied,
Lust still had rioted and raged on earth,
For beasts and birds were made by nature so,
But jest no more; stem not my passion's tide;
Let hot concupiscence spring now to birth.
And die in sighs that flutter soft and low.
I pray thee act the wanton bold with me,
That both my lance and balls may enter thee.

A Man's Yard

(c. 1600)

Read me a riddle: what is this
You hold in your hand when you piss?
It is a kind of pleasing sting,
A pricking and a pleasing thing;
It is a stiff short fleshly pole
That's fit to stop a maiden's hole;
It is Venus' wanton staying wand,
That ne'er had feet and yet can stand;
It is a pen with a hole in the top,
To write between her two-leaved book;
It is a thing both dumb and blind,
Yet narrow holes in dark can find;
It is a dwarf in height and length,
And yet a giant in his strength.

The Gods
(Unknown Author, American, 1880)

I will tell you a tale of a wondrous convention —
'Twas called by the Gods, in the long, long ago,
But the cause of the call I am sure I can't mention,
I was not of the party and hence I don't know.

In the soft, hazy twilight the members were seated
In elegant drawing-room high in the sky
With nectar ambrosial their bosoms were heated
And Venus sat smiling on Jupiter's thigh.

Now Jupiter — God of the lightning and thunder —
Of Cupid's bold pranks was the sport and the brunt,
'Neath the clothes of sweet Venus he thrust his hand under
And to her astonishment tickled her cunt.

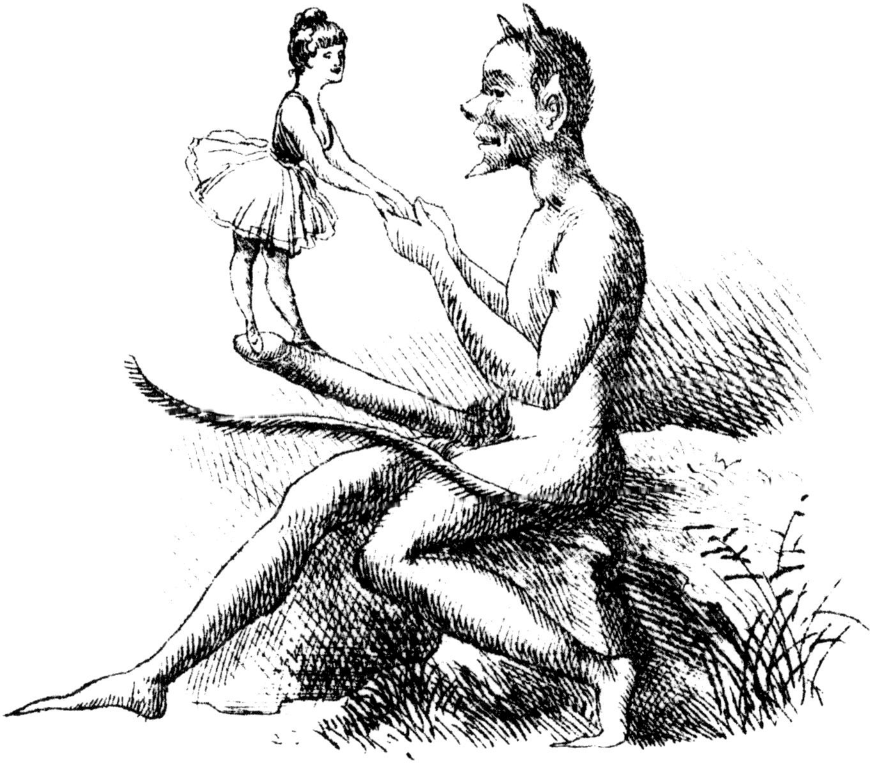

Ma commère quand je danse

The Gods

CONTINUED

This conduct the she-gods outspokenly blamed,
And said that such actions they never could be stand.
Poor Venus — she blushed, hung her head, looked ashamed,
And to his astonishment spent in his hand.

Gay Mercury now felt a strong inclination,
And pulled up some half-dozen Goddesses' frocks,
But each one declined his polite invitation
For fear that he'd give 'em the clap or the pox.

Esculapius said he'd examine his dodger,
But swore that he never would do it on tick.
And Mercury being a dollarless codger
The physician refused to examine his prick.

Now Neptune — the God of the rivers and ditches,
Felt the fire of Cupid distilled through his bones,
So without more ado he unbuttoned his breeches
And just commenced picking the crabs off his stones.

Mars went up to Juno and swore upon honor
He'd make it all right and she'd nothing to fear.
He settled the question by mounting upon her
And into her thrust the whole length of his spear.

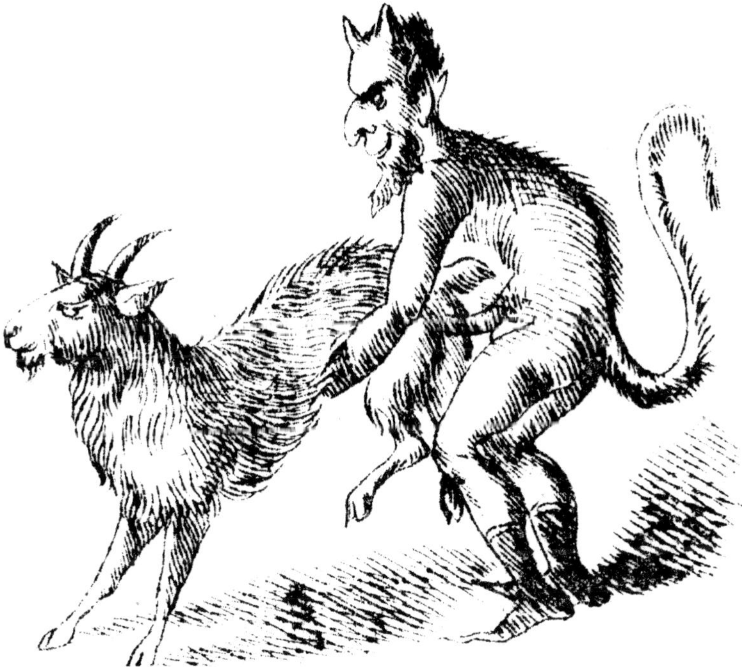

Jouissance Diabolique

The Gods

CONTINUED

Poor Juno, alarmed at his heated condition,
Now gently endeavored his lust to control.
But burning with passion he tore the partition
That parted her quiff from her dirty arse-hole.

Apollo his lyre now ceased to be playing,
And into a nook pretty Hebe he led.
The God was too hot to waste time in delaying
And quickly the damsel was placed on the bed.

In the midst of this strange mythological crisis
Adonis — a regular dandified buck —
Tipped up on the floor the sweet creature called Isis
And gave her a most systematical fuck.

Old Vulcan — the blacksmith — came in with a swagger,
And swore in the rodgering he'd take a part.
He instantly pulled out his old tallawagger
And then let a most diabolical fart.

The disgusted of the party, and Castor and Pollox —
Minions of Jupiter, handsome and rich —
Grabbed hold of the cuss by the neck and the ballocks
And chucked out the nasty old son of a bitch.

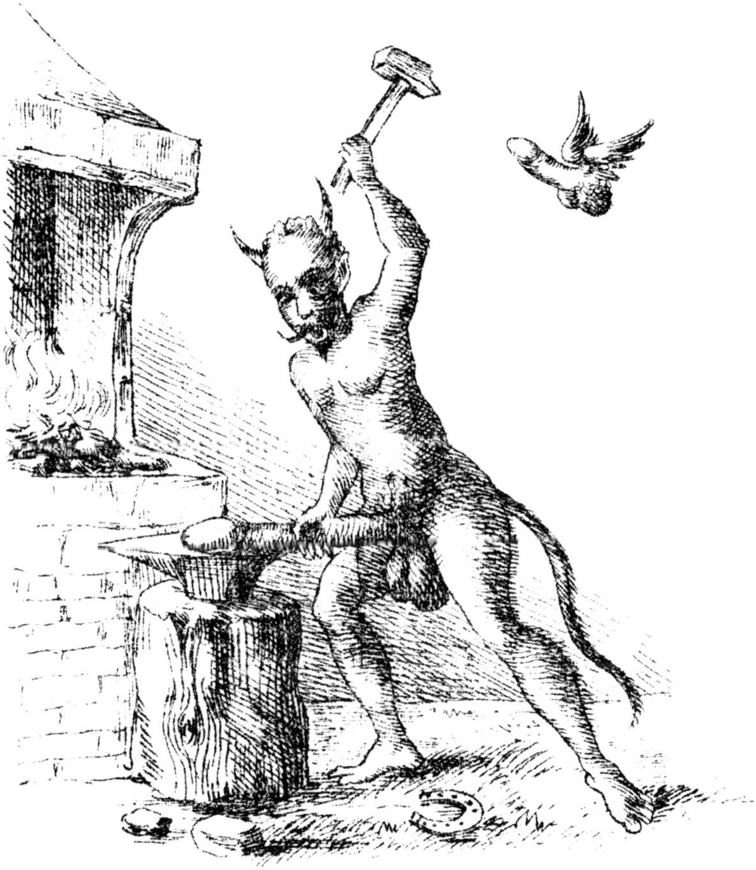

Chienne de pine!

The Gods

CONTINUED

Old Saturn, fierce Jupiter's sire, inspected
The charms that were hidden 'neath Niobe's frock,
But the impudent nymph took a shit unexpected
And wiped off her arse on his limber old cock.

Minerva came in filled with love and desire,
And her month being over she took off the rag,
Then impelled by the pressure of Cupid's bright fire
She went up to Bacchus and asked for a shag.

To him then she offered her matronly treasure,
And in his breeches she thrust her fair hand,
But the goddess of wisdom was grieved beyond measure
To find him so drunk his prick wouldn't stand.

Then Somnus and Morpheus — guardians of sleep —
O'er the passionate group threw a somnolent cloak,
And sadly and silently sat down to weep,
For no holes had been left where their peckers could soak.

This over-true tale of the Mythical Gods
Show them up as a lustful lascivious set
They gave up all else for the sake of their cods,
And for all that we know they are going it yet.

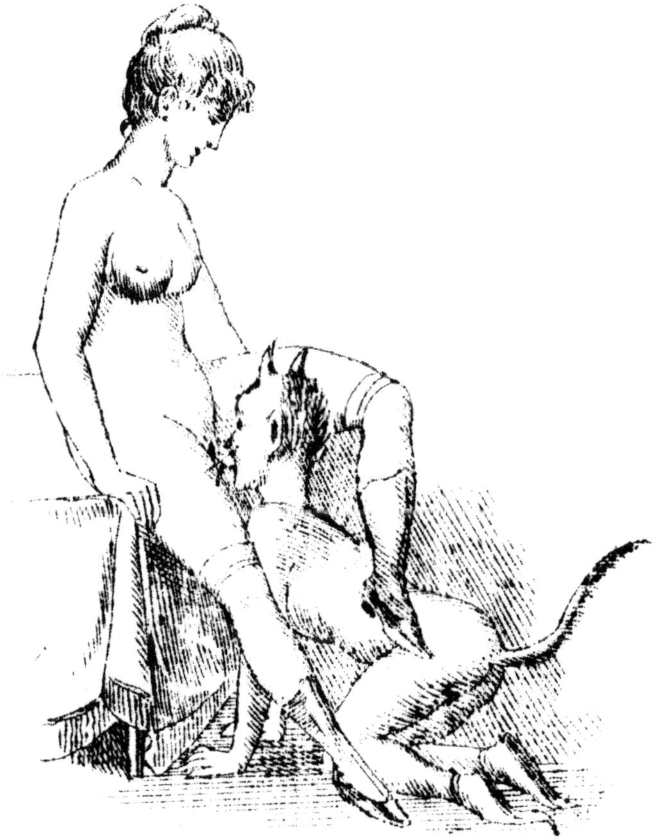

Doucement! doucement!

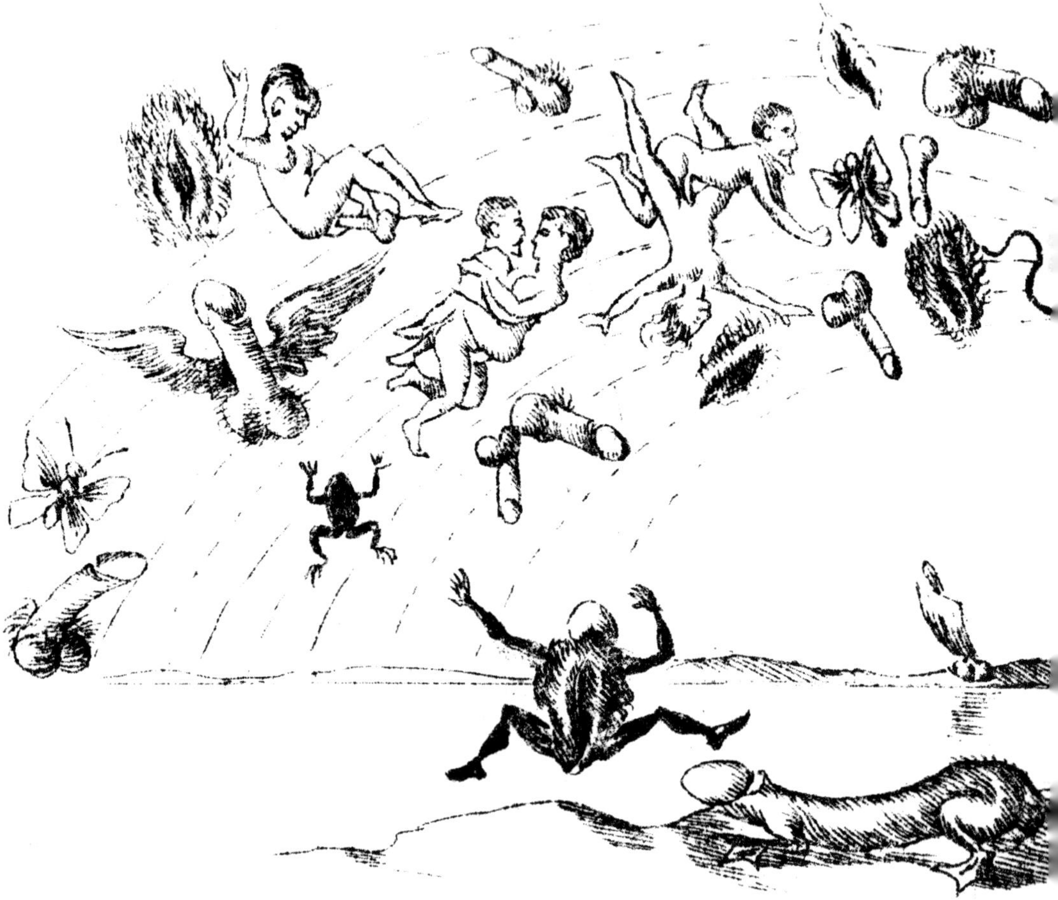

La Rosée Diabolique.

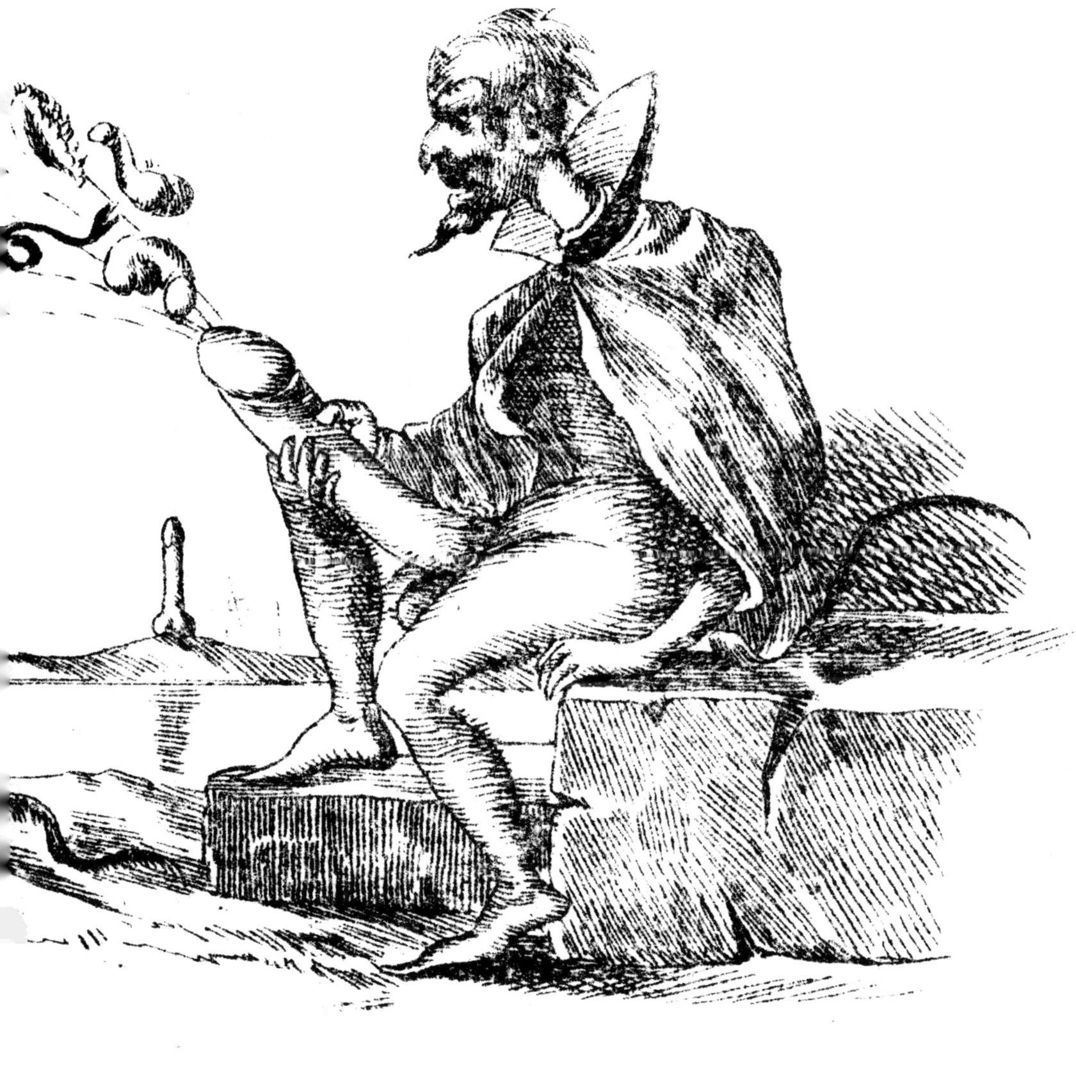

Concerning Pricks

By Lady Fanny Woodcock

Lepoittevin's art depicting the Devil and sundry demons with enormous and engorged phalli speaks to a subset of erotica enjoyed by both men and women—the humorous. Dissecting both human sexuality and amatory depictions in visual and written forms is beyond the scope of what *Bawdy Tales* wishes to do. Still, we hope that knowing more about the history of dirty books adds a frisson to your enjoyment of this robust selection of writings gathered for your delectation.

Excavations in Pompeii revealing crude penis graffiti show us a truism in all humor in that we tend to laugh at our excesses. *The Satyricon* (c. 60 ACE) by Petronius Arbiter is one of the earliest documented sexualized works of Western fiction and is the satirical tale of a man cursed by Priapus to impotence. It details his sexual failures and misery as he encounters progressively outrageous sexual scenes which he is doomed to never enjoy. It is the exaggeration of the depiction that makes it funny. Applied to the seventeenth to nineteenth centuries' bawdy writings, the more excessive, the more extreme, the more outlandish the characterization of a sexual encounter or the sexual act, the funnier it was to the reader. Of course, there is a large body of sexualized writing from the era that was wholly intended to titillate and excite readers. Just as there is also a subset of erotica that is disguised political critique.

Sexualized writing, no matter how humorous, was considered pornographic by governments in Western Europe and later, the United States, and subject to restrictive laws. Literary attempts to depict sexuality were subject to confiscation, and the authors and publishers were imprisoned. The true dawning of erotic literature begins in the sixteenth

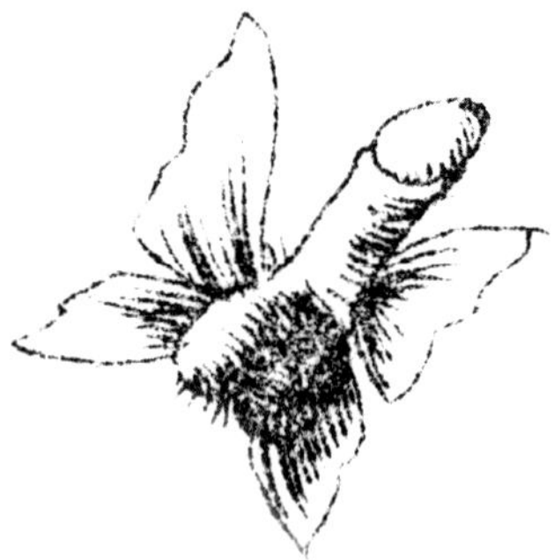

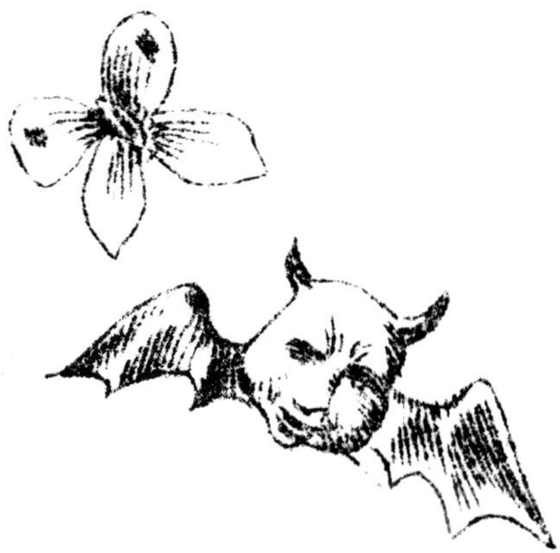

century, and its growth coincides with the technological advances of the printing press. Travel amongst the upper classes and trade between European countries made the exchange of newly printed works relatively easy to acquire and sell dirty books.

The style of erotica in the 1600–1700s was braggadocio tales of conquest, outsized exploits of rakes and libertines, and long poetic tales of ribald antics of royalty and commoner alike. No one embodied this spirit more than John Rochester, the 2nd Earl of Wilmot, whose legend was writ large in the years 1663–80s through a combination of his antics and writing, before dying of a stew of venereal diseases at age thirty-three. Rochester was exiled from English court life a few times—not for the sexual content but the veiled criticism of King Charles II. (Rochester's "Signior Dildo" is included here.)

Italy and France led the way in the creation and printing of erotica in the 1700s. The books of this era have distinct stylistic features that separate them from the previous generation. Where earlier erotica was either images or text, the new crop of books combined images and text. Sometimes the images were intended to complement the text, as in the case for the popular "dialogues" that pretend to be an

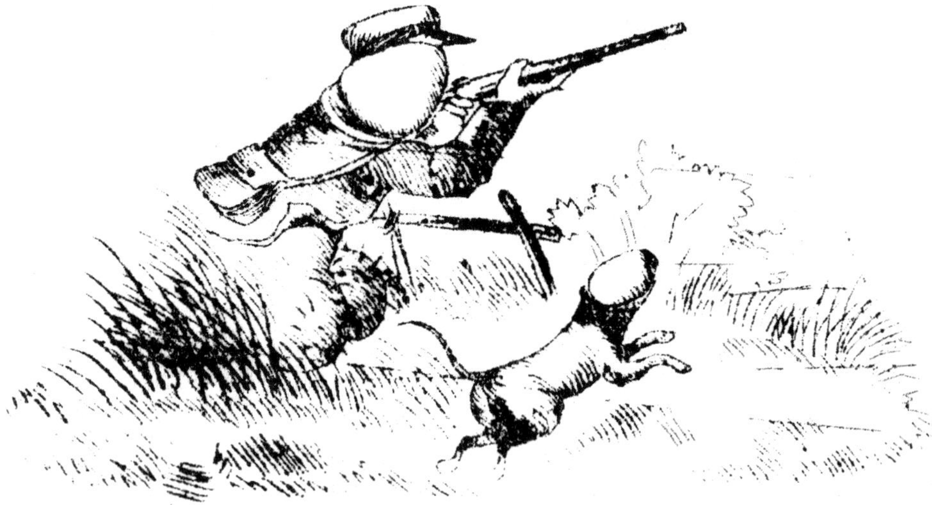

Il y est.

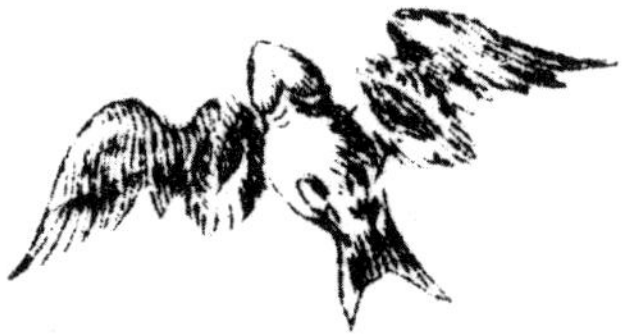

instructional from an experienced libertine to a virginal acolyte. This style of erotica was so pervasive that the structure was used by de Laclos in his 1782 novel, *Les Liaisons dangereuses* (*Dangerous Liaisons*). De Laclos' book was considered scandalous due to his depiction of the aristocratic classes' amoral debauchery and not for the sexual content. He was, as were de Sade and Restif de la Bretonne, using sexual depravity as a stand-in for social and political corruption.

The other distinct style of erotica to come from the eighteenth entury was the anti-clerical tales of randy priests and insatiable nuns. We know that the Italian pornographer, Aretino, enjoyed the patronage of Cardinal Hippolyte de' Medici, who interceded on his behalf with Pope Clement when he was outraged by his books of "positions" and that many of the wealthy French and Italian prelates were political appointees rather than men of God. But after the Protestant Reformation, a new audience for tales of ecclesiastical erotica was found among the anti-Rome, anti-Papist Germans and English. These books often feature stories of victimized women who endure the sexual attentions of cloistered nuns, and depict convents and monasteries as depraved dens of iniquity. Beyond the titillation factor, these stories mocked the Church and her known hypocrisies. Many of the tales of rogue priests and nuns are quite funny because, again, the outrageous antics which end in a comeuppance of the religious figures succeeded in mocking and defanging the moral authority of the Church.

In England, the Society for the Suppression of Vice was formed in 1802 with a broad remit to monitor brothels, atheistic meetings, public cursing, and of course, dirty books. Beyond the influx of imported erotica, the first sexualized novel written in English caused a sensation. John Cleland's *Fanny Hill*[1], or more accurately, *Memoirs of a Woman of Pleasure*, was published in 1748 and has remained in print ever since. The plot reflects the popular style of the day as it purports to be the true story of a wealthy lady born poor

1 "Fanny" is English slang for the vulva.

who literally slept her way to the top. Though the English word "fuck" had been in use for centuries, Cleland does not use explicit words to describe sexual acts but relies on euphemisms and slang, which, consequently, introduces that slang to readers. The book was, of course, banned in England, but that didn't prevent savvy publishers from pirating multiple versions.

Fanny Hill also has the honor of being the first book banned in the United States. The young country relied on religious leaders to enforce moral codes and, for the most part, allowed the few printers publishing erotica freedom to enjoy their First Amendment rights. But its republic system of states meant that individual states could ban printed materials. Massachusetts prohibited the printing and sale of *Memoirs of a Woman of Pleasure* in 1821. (Though it pays to note that the first book burning was also in Massachusetts in 1650 and was a reaction to a political treatise challenging the Puritans' religious authority.) Regardless of where printed, the illicit nature of the erotic book business set up the conditions for a secretive black market. Because publishers (who were often also the printers) bore the legal risk when printing and disseminating sexualized

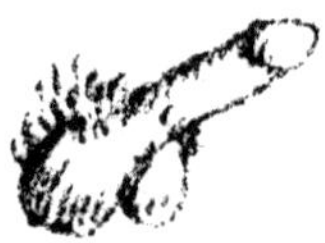

material, they became adept at circumventing the moral and legal authorities.

Print technologies in the 1800s were quickly innovating, which increased the volume while decreasing the cost of printing and publishing. Pirated copies of hundred-year-old lithographs and stories flooded the erotic book trade, leading to the explosion of books and magazines devoted to sex during the early Victorian era. There were two types of publishers: those who would print anything if it were lucrative, and those who were aficionados and supporters of erotic literature. The naughty book business' clandestine nature also ensured that copyright laws were readily discarded—noms de plume, usually of a ridiculous nature, disguised actual authorship. Publication dates and locations were obscured. Books printed in French would be hastily and poorly translated into English by London publishers. One printer/publisher's success with a title ensured that others would create a version with a slightly different title to capitalize on the popularity. The most famous and most reprinted novel is the French book *Histoire de Dom Bougre, Portier des Chartreux*[2], an anti-clerical "autobiography"

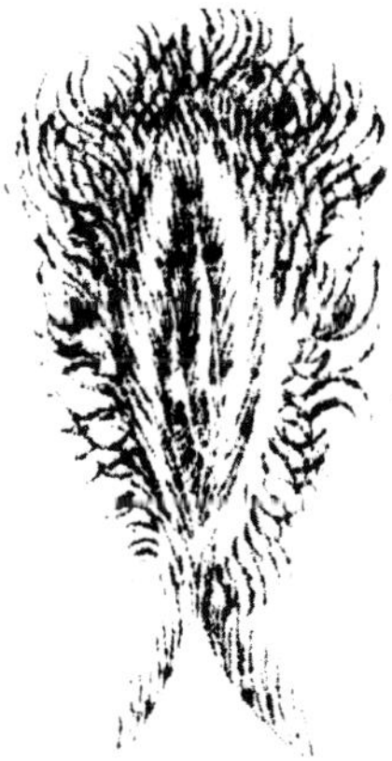

2 The title is a French rhyming slang joke. In English would be History of Father Bugger, Doorkeeper of the Monastery.

of a priest. English printers translated and reworked the text as it first appeared in 1801 as *The Adventures of Silas Shovewell* and later as *Father Silas*, *Brother Silas*, and other variations. This copycat publishing went on in Europe until the Obscene Publications Act of 1857 in England resulted in a crackdown. To be a connoisseur and collector of printed erotica meant reading multiple versions of the same story.

While the English morality laws meant that erotica wasn't available to most readers, elite collectors developed relationships with a favored printer/publisher and would sponsor the creation of privately printed erotica. The sponsor might offer copies to his fellow connoisseur, or the ambitious publisher established an ongoing subscription service. The period between the 1860s to the early 1900s sees the production of erotic books with exquisitely rendered lithographs, gold leafing, and quality Morocco bindings intended for wealthy and astute collectors who wanted more than the cheap offerings available to the middle-class buyers. As a privately printed book, it would escape the strictures of the obscenity law. We have these aristocratic collectors to thank for preserving centuries of pornographic works. (Though

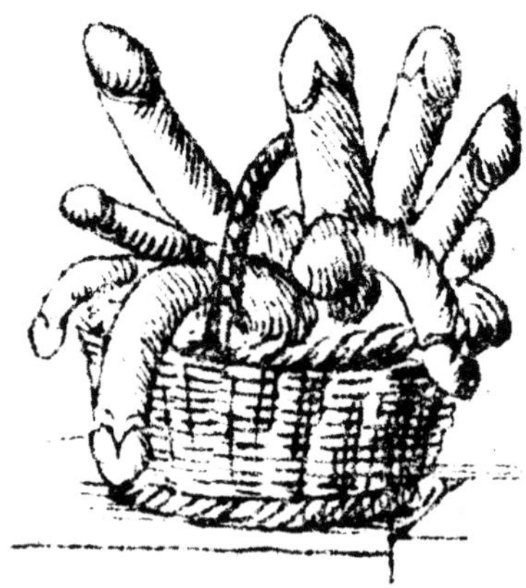

the British Library and France's National Library began collecting and documenting the books in the mid-1800s in the name of scholarship. These books were not for public consumption but locked away in the Private Case of the British Library and L'Enfer in the Bibliotheque nationale du France. The Private Case stopped acquiring material in 1990 and is now accessible to the public.)

But there is a single British, Victorian-era collector who stands out in this regard because of his obsessive thoroughness—Henry Spencer Ashbee. Using the pseudonym 'Pisanus Fraxi,' Ashbee compiled three volumes of extensive bibliographies that sought to catalog every single pornographic title ever printed. (Though he includes a few books of "orientalism," his focus is primarily on Western literature.) Ashbee's bibliographies, published between 1877 to 1885, were initially organized by title, with the later editions catalogued by subject matter. Ashbee's Indexes were far more than listings of titles. Each entry contained notes about the work, including plot summaries, research on the author, and a history of previous editions and versions. His collection was bequeathed to the British National Museum, who kept the "literature" and consigned the obscene material to the Private Case at the British Library.

Ashbee was part of a small group of European collectors who traded material and then began writing and commissioning 'privately printed' works. Ashbee is also thought to be the author of the Victorian classic *My Secret Life* (1888), whose first edition was limited to twenty-five copies printed by August Brancart, a Belgian publisher credited with bringing many translated French titles to English readers. Other French and Belgian publishers began publishing books in English for the export market to exploit a loophole in English law: English-language books published in France were not subject to censorship.

The developments of offset printing and paperback binding in the late 1800s and early 1900s resulted in cheap, quickly produced books. Many of these books made their way to soldiers fighting in the U.S. Civil War and were known as "barracks favorites" but the lack of literacy among the poor, conscripted troops made erotic photographs more popular than books. Post-Civil War, many people were appalled at the pornography, drug addiction, and

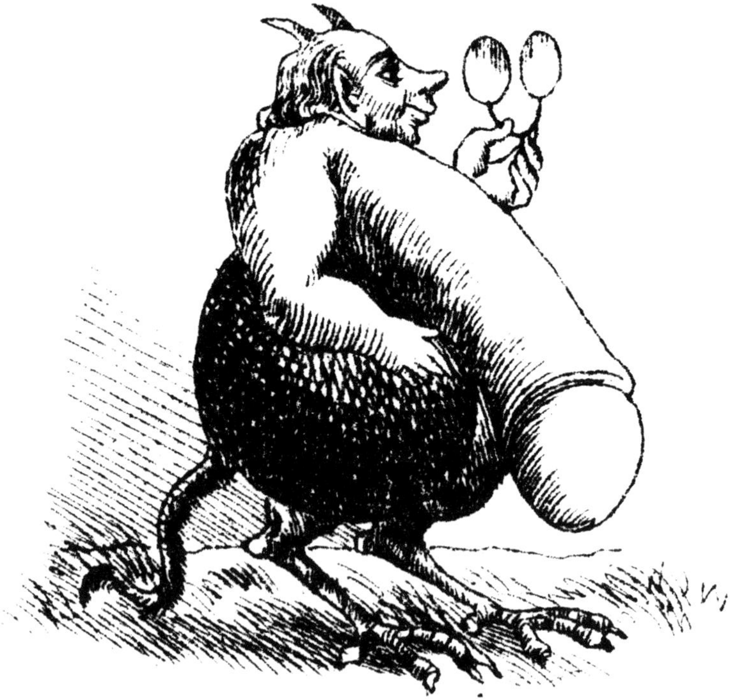

Phénomène vivant.

atheism brought home by war-damaged veterans. Evangelical crusaders began working to stamp out all forms of vice and succeeded when the United States enacted the Comstock Act in 1873 that forbids the sending of obscene materials via the United States Postal Service. Erotic books, pictures and "sex toys" as well as information on birth control, contraceptives, and abortifacients and items related to those topics were all considered obscene under Comstock.

These laws tamped down local production of pornographic books but did not prevent the next wave of soldiers returning from the battlefields from bringing back thousands of cheap French paperbacks after World War I. The first obscenity trial concerning printed pornography was brought against the *Little Review Magazine* in 1920 for printing the Nausicaa chapter of James Joyce's *Ulysses*. The modernists won the day but not the total repeal of the Comstock Laws. In fact, sex researcher Alfred Kinsey's set of Lepoittevin's lithographs were seized by the U.S. Postal Service under Comstock in 1956. It is not until 1959, when Barney Rosset's Grove Press prevails in the obscenity trial brought against them for their unexpurgated edition of D.H. Lawrence's 1928 book *Lady Chatterley's Lover*, do publishers fully enjoy freedom to print erotica. *Bawdy Tales* is an homage to the anonymous and not so anonymous writers and publishers who saw the joy in human sexuality. •

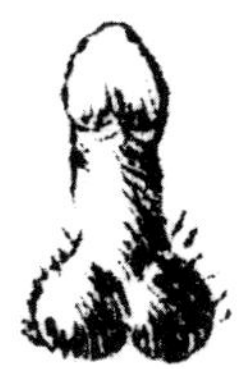

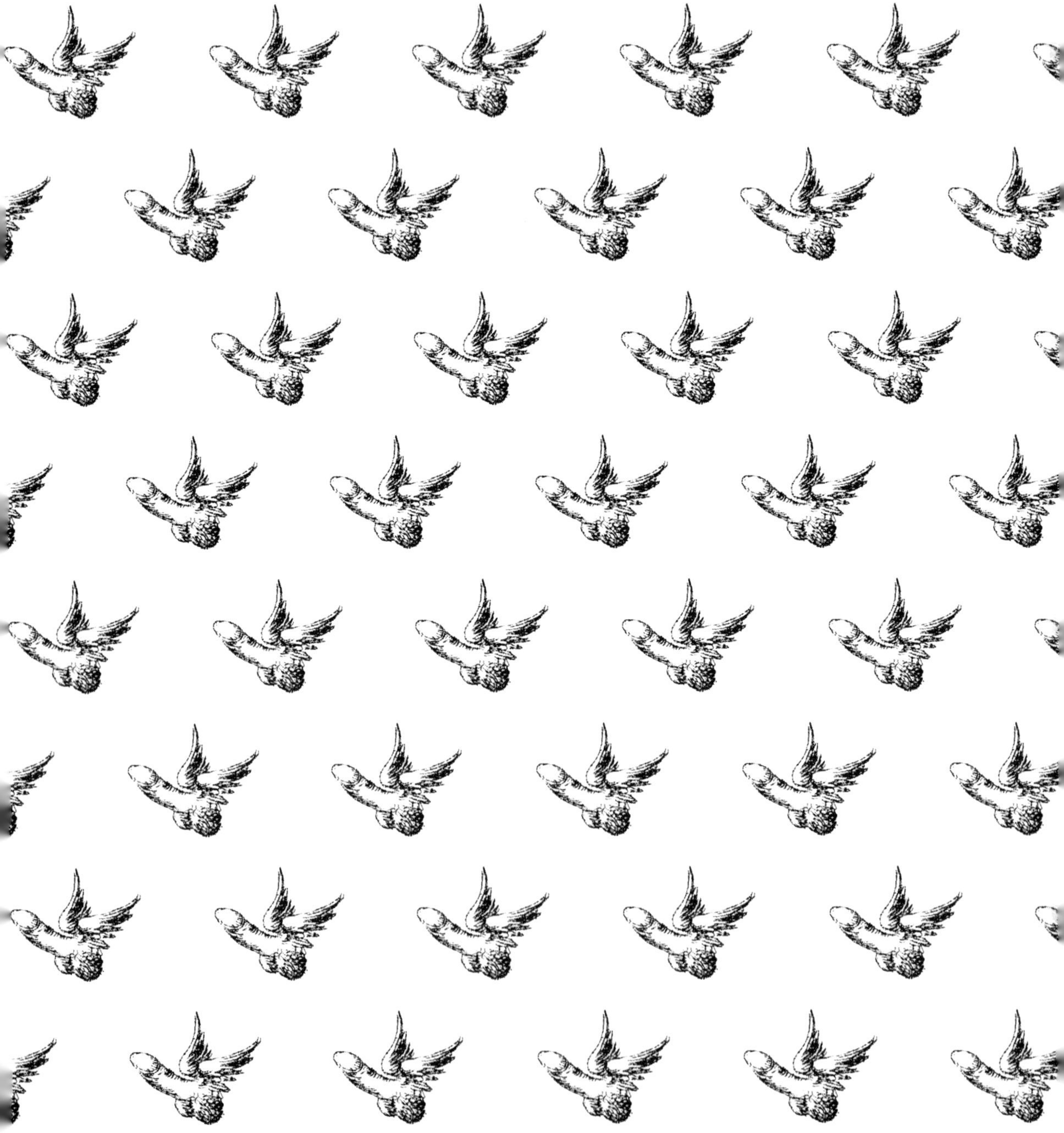

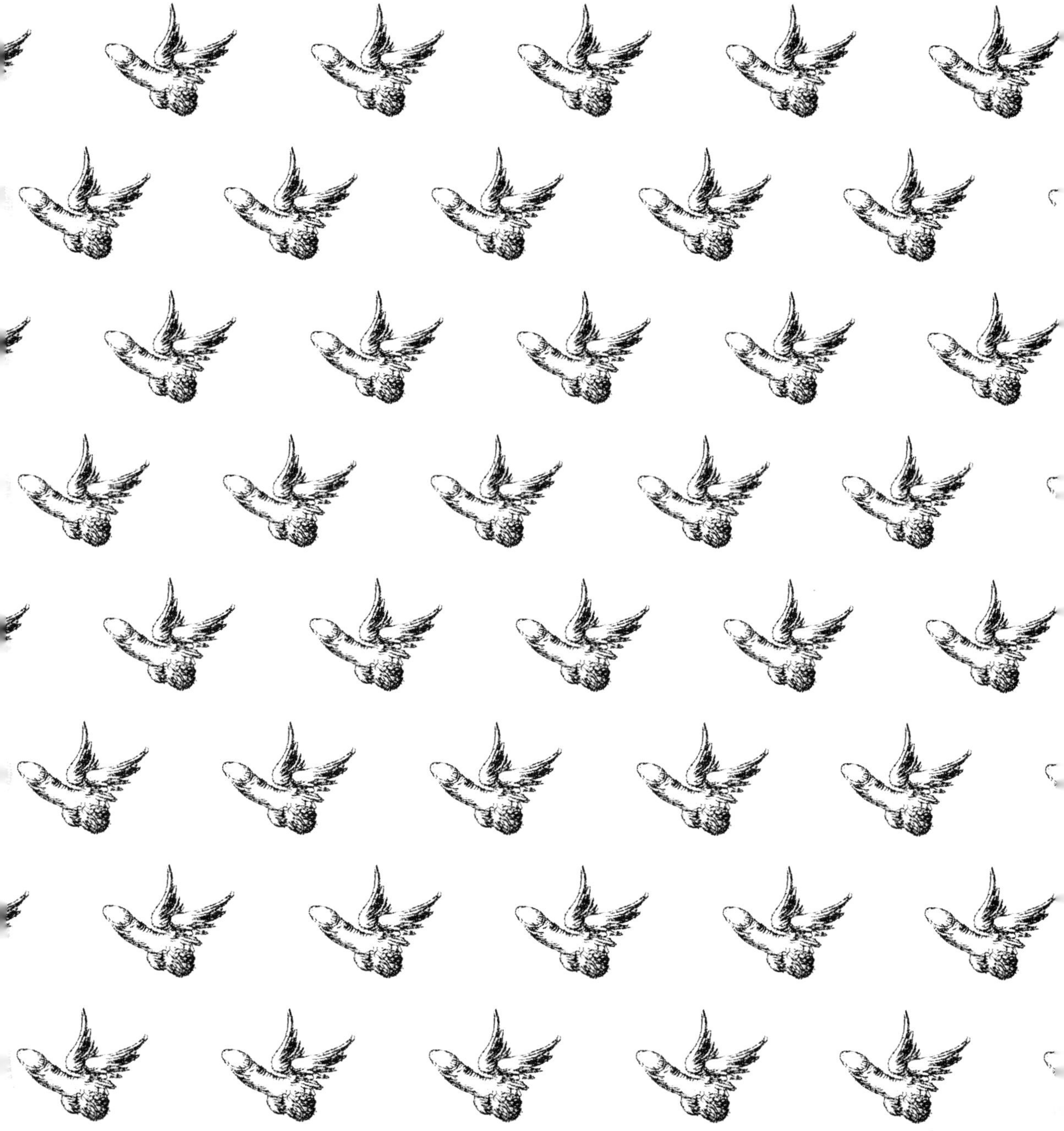

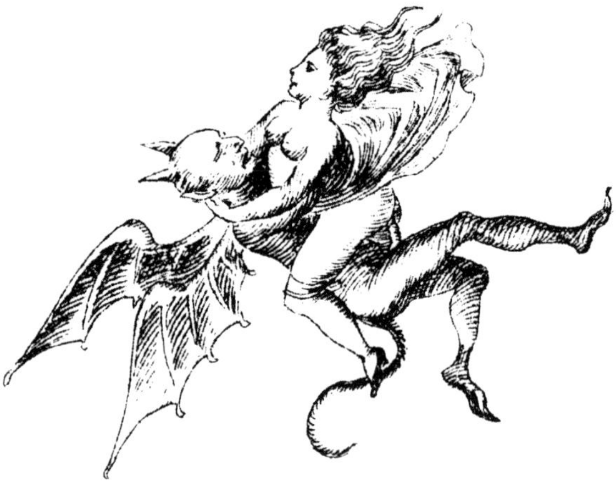

"By my life, this is my lady's hand. These be her very C's, her U's and her T's, and thus makes she her great P's."

(Malvolio, *Twelfth Night*, Act 2, Scene 5)

Sex, since its conception, is funny. A wicked sense of humor is sexually attractive. To wit: *Bawdy Tales and Trifles of Devilries for Ladies and Gentlemen of Experience*. Enjoy this tome of rare humorous illustrations by 18th-century French artist Eugène Lepoittevin coupled with an arousing selection of ribald jokes, puns, and poems curated from hidden collections of vintage erotica.

Lepoittevin's drawings were banned by the United States until the early 1960s, and *Bawdy Tales* is the first U.S. collection in print since the early 1900s. Art lovers and erotica aficionados alike will appreciate this collection of rarities. Also features essays by art historian Dr. Sarah Lea Burns on Lepoittevin and his art and Lady Fanny Woodcock on the history of erotic books.

$36.95

ISBN 978-1-62731-119-9

53695>

9 781627 311199